Everything Happens to Me

Peter Cherches

Everything Happens to Me by Peter Cherches
978-1-949790-88-7   Paperback
978-1-949790-89-4   Ebook

Cover image generated by Bing Image Creator from a prompt
    by Peter Cherches.
Layout and book design by Mark Givens
First Pelekinesis Printing 2024

For information:

Pelekinesis
112 Harvard Ave #65
Claremont, CA 91711 USA

Library of Congress Cataloging-in-Publication Data

Names: Cherches, Peter, author.
Title: Everything happens to me / Peter Cherches.
Description: Claremont, CA : Pelekinesis, 2024. | Summary: "This episodic
    novel chronicles the trials and tribulations of Peter Cherches, an
    obscure Brooklyn writer who suffers the slings and arrows of outrageous
    tormentors, most notably his next-door neighbor. Cherches's world is
    overrun with doppelgängers, doppelgängers' doppelgängers, malevolent
    technology, masks, doubts, and unreliable mirrors. Think of this as a
    kinder and gentler Book of Job, with New York attitude and borscht belt
    humor, as well as echoes of Kafka, Borges, and Serling. Rarely has one
    man's misery been so much fun"-- Provided by publisher.
Identifiers: LCCN 2024001821 (print) | LCCN 2024001822 (ebook) | ISBN
    9781949790887 (Paperback) | ISBN 9781949790894 (Ebook)
Subjects: LCGFT: Psychological fiction. | Novels.
Classification: LCC PS3553.H3527 E94 2024 (print) | LCC PS3553.H3527
    (ebook) | DDC 813/.54--dc23/eng/20240117
LC record available at https://lccn.loc.gov/2024001821
LC ebook record available at https://lccn.loc.gov/2024001822

www.pelekinesis.com

Everything Happens to Me

Peter Cherches

To Brooklyn!

Grateful acknowledgment is made to the following journals in which portions of this book originally appeared:

10 by 10 Flash, 365 Tomorrows, 50 Word Story, Book Post, The Cafe Irreal, Danse Macabre, Flash Boulevard, Fleas on the Dog, Heavy Feather Review, Impspired, Litro, Lotus Eater, Maryland Literary Review, The Odd Magazine, The Pine Cone Review, South Florida Poetry Journal, Synchronized Chaos, Terror House, A Thin Slice of Anxiety, Tiny Molecules, Unlikely Stories, Wigleaf.

The following chapters previously appeared in *Whistler's Mother's Son* in different form and context: 5, 8, 36, 45, 65.

Contents

1

Pot Luck

My next-door neighbor was throwing a little party, a get-together, a pot luck. He couldn't very well exclude me since the whole building was invited, so I made my signature pot luck dish, a simple but popular potato salad made from halved boiled new potatoes, skin on, dressed with tarragon mustard, mayonnaise, and capers.

I put some pants on and rang the bell next door. One of the guests, another neighbor, opened the door with a chicken drumstick in her right hand. I knew her face, but not her name. "Come on in and join the festivities," she said.

I introduced myself. "Pete," I said, and extended my right hand to shake as I balanced the bowl in my left hand against my chest. She shifted the drumstick to her left hand and shook my clean, dry, recently washed right hand with her greasy one.

"Tanya. You live right next door, right, Pete?"

"Right," I said. "I share a wall with this apartment."

"I've heard," she said.

What did she hear? What did the neighbor tell her?

"Oh?" I said.

"Yes indeedy. Your next-door neighbor and I have no secrets from each other!"

Was it something that could count as a secret? What could the neighbor have heard?

"Some pretty amusing stuff, I've got to say," she added.

Amusing? Do I talk in my sleep, loudly enough for the neighbor to hear? Does he have access to my unconscious, an access even greater than mine? I needed to find out what the neighbor heard. Should I be blunt, get right to the point, or would it be wiser to start by fishing around?

I decided to cast my line and see what bit. "Amusing?"

"Surely you wouldn't disagree."

"Well," I said, "I've never really thought about it."

"Are you serious?"

"Sure I'm serious. Why shouldn't I be serious?"

"Well," she said, "it's just that it's really funny to a third party, to be honest. No offense."

It must have been pretty funny to a second party too, if the neighbor told her about it.

"I guess I'd have to hear it through your ears," I said, hoping she'd get the hint.

"I guess you would," she replied. "Well, have a good time. This chicken's really good, by the way. The old Greek lady in 2B made it. I don't know what these herbs are, but it's so yummy." She walked away.

I found a table to drop my potato salad bowl on and picked up a drumstick. Tanya was right. Yummy.

Then the neighbor, my next-door neighbor, that is, saw me and came over. "Welcome to my humble abode," he said. "Are you having a good time?"

"Well, I just got here." Then I said, "I'm glad I decided not to skip this shindig and stay in my apartment. With all this crowd noise it would be pretty hard to get anything done, what with the thin walls and all."

"Thin walls? I've never noticed. Well, have fun, and get yourself a glass of Zinfandel before it's all gone." He walked away, and soon I saw him whispering conspiratorially into Tanya's ear.

"Mrs. Papadopoulos!" I said as the lady from 2B came toward me. "Your drumsticks are delicious."

2

First Sale

I was waiting for the shop to open. I waited in front of the security-gated entrance. Then the shopkeeper, a short, stout woman in her fifties with rust-colored fly-away hair and a devilish glint in her eye came by and turned the key to get the electric gate lifter going. "Another op'nin', another show," she said as the gate noisily rose. Then she unlocked the door.

"First customer of the day," she said. "Gotta make a sale. It's good luck. You're gonna have a good day if you make a sale to the first customer."

"Well, let's see what we can do," I said.

"How 'bout one of these," she said, laying an item I had absolutely no use for on the counter.

"I can't say I need one of those," I said.

"How about the little lady? You'd score points big time."

"There is no lady, little, medium, or large," I said. "I'm single."

"All right," she said, "let's try something else." She walked a few steps and brought something down from a shelf. "How about this? Can't go wrong with one of these."

"Not my style," I said, which was the truth.

"Well, well," she said, "aren't we the tough customer!"

The next thing she showed me was small and fragile. "The genius thing about this is it'll fit anywhere," she said.

"I'm always breaking things. It wouldn't last a week."

She didn't look too happy. I heard a little sigh.

"What do you want, the shirt off my back?" Then she started unbuttoning her blouse. She took it off and held it out to me as she stood there in her bra and fleshy midriff. "Here. Take it. You can have it cheap. Name your price."

I was taken aback. She was making me uncomfortable. I wanted to get out of there. I figured I should make her an offer, to make her happy. "How about five bucks?"

"Five bucks! Do you realize this is genuine viscose?"

I was ashamed. "Twenty?"

"Keep guessin'."

"Fifty?"

"You're getting warmer. Double that and you've got a deal."

I handed her a c-note. "You're quite a persuasive salesperson," I said.

"I have my moments," she said. Then she started folding the shirt. "Will a bag do, or do you need a box?"

"Neither," I said. "I'll wear it now." She handed me the shirt and I put it on. It took me a while to button up. It was an awkward fit, but I figured maybe my old Orchard Street tailor could make something of it.

"A pleasure doing business with you. Wear it in good health."

3

The Cat Burglar

A cat burglar crawled through my bedroom window in the middle of the night, waking me from troubled dreams. I gasped as I bolted up in bed and saw the figure halfway into my apartment. He made his way through and landed on his feet in front of the window.

"Shhh," he said. "If you do as you're told, nothing will happen to you. Keep your voice down. If you have something to say, say it sotto voce."

He had a black stocking over his head, like the ones that bank robbers in movies often wear. He was wearing a black T-shirt, black sweatpants, and black joggers.

"Listen," I said in a stage whisper, "I don't keep too much cash in the apartment, but there's maybe eighty bucks in my wallet, and some loose change." Then I thought of something else. "Oh, and I also have some foreign currency—Euros, British pounds, Mexican pesos. If I think I might return to a country I hold on to the leftover cash from my last trip. There's probably about three, four hundred dollars worth."

"I don't want your money!" He sounded offended.

What else could he want? "Take my TV, then, or my stereo system."

"I'm not here for consumer electronics."

"Are you hungry?" I asked. "I could make you a sandwich."

"That's very kind of you," he said, "but I already had a burger and fries. As a matter of fact, it was at that little French place in

Windsor Terrace you like so much."

"Le Paddock?"

"Yeah. I had it just the way you like it, with Gruyère and bacon, medium-rare."

"Wait a minute, how do you know how I like my burgers, and where?"

"Give me a little credit, dude! I do my research."

Why was he researching my culinary preferences? How would this help him achieve his criminal purposes, whatever they may be?

"Well, what do you want from me, then?"

"Want? I want to understand!"

"To understand? To understand what?"

"Everything. I want to understand roots, and causes, and effects."

"Are you talking about the meaning of life? Are you trying to find out why you're here?"

"No, you moron, I'm not trying to find out why I'm here!" He sounded angry. There was a long silence. Then he spoke again.

"I'm trying to find out why *you're* here."

4

Unfamiliar Ground

I woke up on a bus I did not remember boarding. It was daylight. My neck was stiff. I looked out the window. The surroundings were unfamiliar. The foliage was unfamiliar, trees and plants I had never seen before. The signs on the shops were in a foreign language. One shop had a painting of a man in an apron chasing a pig with a meat cleaver. The man had a crazed look in his eyes. The pig was wearing sunglasses. The sign said "Klenstarfig." The bus driver called to me. In a thick accent he said, "Sir, you tell me alert you as we approach your stop. Your stop is next one." I sat up straight and looked around, at the empty seat next to me and the rack above. I didn't seem to have any luggage or personal effects, only what I was wearing. "Is your stop," the driver said. I thanked him and got off.

Across the road from the bus stop was a large red brick building with a sign that read "Klenstarfig Pustali Zintro." This must be where I was headed. I walked across the street to the building. I was stopped by a guard. "Nimo?" he asked. I guessed that meant name, so I told him mine. He checked his clipboard and when he found my name he waved me in. I entered the building. A man in an apron said, "Nimo?"

"Peter Cherches," I said. He handed me a pair of overalls.

"Inglis?"

"Yes," I said.

"Apron come later," he said.

I looked around. There were no pigs in sight.

"Where are the pigs?" I asked the man.

He started laughing, a bellowing belly laugh. "War peeg! War peeg, he say!" He pointed toward a door and said, "You!"

I walked through the door. There was a cubicle with my name on it. I saw a computer on the desk. I changed into my overalls and logged in. A message popped up on the screen: Valku, Peter Cherches.

I breathed a sigh of relief. I was back on familiar ground.

5

Passed Out

As I left my building for a walk one Saturday morning, I saw a bunch of people standing around in a circle, looking down at the pavement. I figured whatever it was, there were enough people to take care of it, no need for another gawker, but still I was curious.

"What happened?" I asked a woman as I went to join the circle.

"I don't know, he was just lying there."

I wondered who it was. Perhaps one of my neighbors? It was, after all, right in front of my building. I couldn't get a good look at the guy until I moved further into the circle. Then I saw who it was. It was me!

What was the meaning of this? How was I lying unconscious in front of my building and looking at myself from above at the same time? I was wearing the same clothes, the unconscious me and the conscious me. The standing, conscious me had no memory of anything happening to myself that could have caused me to be lying on the pavement.

"Does anybody know his name?" someone called out.

"Yes," I said, "it's me! Peter Cherches!"

"Peter Cherches? That's a funny name for a dog," someone else said.

Dog? I thought. Then I took another look. It was a big, mangy, stray dog passed out on the sidewalk, not me at all.

Embarrassed, I slunk away from the circle and then ran as fast and as far as my four legs would take me.

6

The Efficiency Expert

I was walking back to my cubicle from the pantry when I noticed a meeting in the fish bowl conference room. Seated in the room were my boss (the head of editorial), her boss (the head of creative), and her boss (the head of marketing), as well as a person I did not recognize at first. Then it hit me. I rubbed my eyes. Yes, I was sure, it was the neighbor! What's he doing here? What business does he have with my management chain of command?

I sat down with my tea and tried to make sense of the situation. Then Susheela, one of my co-workers, came by. She said, "Have you heard about the efficiency expert?"

I wondered if they still used the term "efficiency expert" in Mumbai, where she grew up. A good old no-bullshit term, tells you right where you stand, unlike "management consultant."

"No," I said, "What gives?"

"There are rumors of big cuts coming. They want to make us leaner and meaner."

"I could certainly be leaner," I said, "but I don't think I could be any meaner."

"This is no joke. Nobody's safe," she said.

Least of all me, I thought. Who gives a shit about proofreading in the 21st century?

Was the neighbor the efficiency expert, the management consultant? I was never sure what he did for a living. What a coincidence that of all places he'd be doing his dirty deeds at my place of business. Surely I'd be the first to go. That bastard has a vendetta against me, I was sure. I wouldn't be surprised if he engineered this whole thing himself, just to get me fired from my job, or perhaps to see how I'd grovel under the threat of impending unemployment.

Well I wouldn't grovel, nosiree Bob. I'm close enough to retirement that I could just bite the bullet, maybe freelance a little. I'd have more time for writing. Maybe it's a blessing in disguise.

A few minutes later, my manager came over to my cubicle. Uh oh, I thought, here comes the bad news.

"Hey Pete," she said, "the guy whose company services our printers said you look just like a guy from his apartment building." I knew it, I thought, until my manager added, "But you don't live in Bay Ridge, do you?"

"No, Park Slope."

"I thought so. Well, I guess you have a lookalike in Bay Ridge."

Whew. I dodged a bullet, for the time being at least. So it wasn't the neighbor after all, and it wasn't the efficiency expert.

But what if the efficiency expert rumor were true nonetheless?

Well, at least I'd stand a fighting chance with a total stranger.

7

My Toothbrush

I have one of those talking electric toothbrushes. The kind that tells you your progress. When you power it up, it says, "Hello!" After 30 seconds it says, "First quadrant complete!" The voice is kind of enthusiastic. Definitely a trained voice actor. The first time I heard it I was reminded of the voice on the subway announcements, the guy who says, "Stand clear of the closing doors!" After another 30 seconds it says, "Second quadrant complete!" At the 90-second mark, "Third quadrant complete!" Finally, when two minutes are up, "Fourth quadrant complete! Congratulations!"

It's really not any more helpful than the ones that just buzz every 30 seconds, though some studies say it encourages faithful brushing for a full two minutes.

Anyway, this morning my toothbrush went off script. When I turned it on, it said, "Good morning, Mr. Cherches. Getting a late start, aren't we?" Well, I suppose we were. It was around 11 a.m. It said, "Let's not waste any more time," so I put it in my mouth and started brushing. "Do you have anything you want to tell me?" it asked as I was brushing.

With my mouth full of toothbrush and paste, I mumbled, "No, what would I want to tell you?"

"You'll have to speak up, Mr. Cherches, I can't hear you," it said.

I managed to say, "No, nothing" in a louder voice, though it came out like "Moe, muffin."

"I don't think you're being completely forthcoming," the toothbrush said.

I had no reason to keep secrets from my toothbrush. What was it fishing for? "Own't moe utcher talk 'mout."

"You seriously don't know, Mr. Cherches?"

"Fearioush!"

"We know you're guilty," it said. "We know all."

It must have been a practical joke. Somebody with toothbrush programming skills must have altered the code. I was mildly amused, but it was kind of creepy. Creepy enough that I decided to turn it off. I pressed the power button. "Not so quick, Mr. Cherches," the toothbrush said. I gasped. "We know all," it repeated. "We know what you did."

What did I do? Seriously, I didn't know. "Guilty of what?"

"Don't be coy, Mr. Cherches."

The head was still vibrating, but I was no longer brushing.

I started thinking. What have I done? What could I be guilty of? I came up with a couple of recent possibilities, but they were really nothing, just misunderstandings. I had managed to smooth both incidents over. Maybe something further back, like when I was still working?

"Earlier," the toothbrush said.

It was a mind reader too!

"In school?"

"Earlier."

"When I was a toddler?"

"Earlier."

"When I was a newborn?"

"Earlier."

"In the womb?"

"Earlier."

This toothbrush was making no sense, I thought. It must be broken. I stopped replying, but it kept repeating, "Earlier."

And since I can't turn the power off, I guess it's going to keep vibrating and saying, "Earlier, earlier, earlier" until there's no more charge.

8

My Crisis

I wasn't feeling myself this morning, so I called 911.

The operator said, "911, what's the address of the emergency?"

I wasn't sure how to answer that. "I don't know," I said, "I guess everywhere."

"Everywhere?" the operator asked.

"Well, everywhere I go," I replied.

"What's the problem?" the operator asked.

"I'm not feeling myself today. I mean, I don't feel connected to myself," I said. "That is, I know who I'm supposed to be, I know my name, my past, my history, my friends and loved ones, but I don't feel like that person."

"Oh," she replied, "you're having an identity crisis."

"I guess you could call it that," I said.

"What's your name?" she asked.

"I don't know how to answer that," I said. "I mean, I know my name's Peter Cherches, but I don't feel like Peter Cherches. I can't even imagine what it would be like to feel like Peter Cherches."

"Who do you feel like?" she asked.

Who did I feel like? That was an interesting question. Who did I feel like? I certainly didn't feel like the person I was supposed to be, Peter Cherches. That is, I didn't feel like the memories were mine. If anything, I felt like someone who didn't know who he felt like.

"I'd like to find out who I feel like," I told the operator.

"Well, Mr. Cherches," she said, and it felt so weird being referred to as Mr. Cherches. "Well, Mr. Cherches, I think the best thing I can do for you is connect you with the identity crisis hotline."

There's an identity crisis hotline? Who knew?

"Would that be all right with you?" she asked.

"Yes," I said, "I suppose that would be OK."

"You just hold on a minute, all right?"

"All right."

I waited for my call to transfer. Then I heard the operator's voice again. "Hello, I'm an operator from 911 in Brooklyn, New York. I have a caller I'd like to refer to you. Would that be all right?"

"Yes," the hotline guy replied, "that will be all right."

"All right, Mr. Cherches," the 911 operator said, "is there anything else I can do for you before I leave this call?"

"No," I said. "Thank you for your help." I heard a change in the aural ambience, signaling that the 911 operator had left the conversation.

"Mr. Cherches?" the identity crisis counselor said. "Thank you for reaching out. My name is Rick. How can I help you?"

I told Rick about my problem, about how I wasn't feeling myself. He was very patient and caring. He let me speak and he would only break in to ask pointed questions when I seemed to be rambling, but even then he gave me some leeway. I don't know how long the call lasted, at least a half hour. I told him all about the life of Peter Cherches and how I didn't feel connected to it anymore. He was very understanding, in no way judgmental—the kind of person I would like to be. "Maybe it's just a phase you're going through," he said. "Maybe if you just give yourself some time things will straighten themselves out."

"Maybe," I replied.

"Do you think you'll be OK on your own now? We'll always be here for you if you need us."

"Yeah," I said, "I'll be OK. Thanks for your help." And I hung up.

Maybe one day this nightmare will come to an end. Maybe one day I'll feel like Peter Cherches again. But for the time being, can you please call me Rick?

Now how can I help you?

9

Stoops to Conquer

I live in a relatively affluent, highly literate neighborhood. I like to think I'm highly literate, but I'm certainly not affluent. I bought my apartment before Brooklyn became hip.

One advantage to living in a relatively affluent, highly literate neighborhood, especially one full of brownstones, is that people are always leaving interesting books on their stoops. I like the randomness and serendipity it adds to my reading life. Stoop finds have introduced me to such wonderful contemporary novelists as Julie Otsuka, Ottessa Moshfegh, and the Finnish comic crime writer Antti Tuomainen. I've also caught up on classics like Erskine Caldwell's *Tobacco Road*, Zora Neale Hurston's *Their Eyes Were Watching God*, and Zola's *Thérèse Raquin*, as well as several sixties suspense thrillers by Charlotte Armstrong, a new name to me.

A few months ago I was walking on Montgomery Place, a block I briefly lived on before buying my current apartment. On a brownstone stoop I saw several paperbacks. There was a Cormac McCarthy novel—no thanks, not my bag; *All The King's Men*, a great book I've already read twice; and a few Harlequin-style romances. I figured this stoop was a bust, but then I noticed a copy of my 2016 collection *Autobiography Without Words*.

The title of my book is a metaphor, of course, but when I opened the copy on the stoop it was literally without words. The cover was the same, with a photo of me as an adolescent clowning around with my friends, but the pages inside were blank. Well, not all of them.

After about 20 pages there was handwriting in cursive. It took me a while to get used to the handwriting, but when I was finally able to read the text I saw that it was a bunch of short stories. I read a few and thought they were quite good. Nothing like my writing, mind you, but excellent nonetheless. Truth be told, I thought these stories were better than my own. They were funnier when they were supposed to be funny, and more heartbreaking when they were meant to be heartbreaking. I gleaned that the writer was a man, more or less of my generation. Many of the stories were about childhood, just like mine, but if I thought I had a miserable childhood, it was nothing compared to this guy's. He made Gorky's childhood seem like a walk in the park.

I was baffled. What could have happened?

I figured there must have been a misprint; somehow blank pages were bound in the cover of my book and apparently sold to an unsuspecting reader. Since few bookstores will deign to carry my books these days, most sales are online, so the potential reader couldn't have discovered the problem until the book arrived in the mail.

But why didn't this person return the book for a refund? Did he actually take the title literally?

And what then inspired him to start writing stories on the pages? Don't get me wrong, I think of writing as a form of collaboration with the reader, and I was glad to see this reader actively engaging in that collaboration. I just needed to make my peace with the unexpected situation.

Who was this reader, this writer? Did he live in this brownstone? Should I ring the buzzers and try to find him?

But even if I did find him, what would I say? It might be awkward, no?

I decided to move on. I took the book home and read the rest in one sitting.

I remained baffled, but I decided to put it out of my mind.

Shortly thereafter, I started getting emails from literary magazines. It seemed that whoever wrote these stories had sent them out for publication under my name. There were a few rejections, but most were acceptances, and from more high-profile journals than usually publish my work. Should I inform them that there was a misunderstanding? But why look a gift horse in the mouth? So I let them go to publication. After decades of trying, my name finally appeared in *Granta*, but the biggest coup was surely *The New Yorker*. Friends and acquaintances congratulated me on the new turn my work had taken. But my newfound modicum of fame didn't last very long. After five or six publications, the counterfeit Peter Cherches stories dried up.

Still, maybe I could use this turn of events to my advantage. Maybe some of those journals that had never previously given me the time of day would start publishing my real stories. So I started sending my own work to these top-tier publications.

I got personalized rejections from all of them. Most took the same tack. They thanked me for my continued interest in their publication, but wondered why I had changed my style so drastically from the work they enjoyed so much.

Well, at least I had my fifteen minutes of minor literary fame, I consoled myself.

Then I bought a blank, unlined notebook, wrapped it in the cover of my subsequent book, *Whistler's Mother's Son*, and left it on that stoop on Montgomery Place.

10

Ransom

Someone had slipped a ransom note under my door. Not really a ransom note, I mean it had the look of a ransom note. It was made up of letters cut from newspapers and magazines. It said: DoN'T forgEt TO put ThE SeAt dOWn. I assume it was referring to the toilet seat. But I'm a guy, and I live alone. Why should I put the seat down? Who would leave me such a note? And why the cut-out letters? It's not as if a potential felony were being committed.

I contemplated the note. I thought I might try to figure out where the letters came from. That's what the detectives do, right, to figure out who the perpetrator might be? Perhaps the source of the letters could offer a clue. I looked more closely. Some of the letters were on yellowed old newsprint, some on newish newsprint, and some from glossy magazines. I couldn't get to first base with those clues.

Maybe there are fingerprints. Should I take it to the police station? But what's the crime? It was phrased as a reminder, not a threat. It didn't say, "Don't forget to put the seat down or else." Would I be laughed out of the police station? That's what they do to white people, right, laugh us out of the police station? They wouldn't shoot me for wasting their time, would they? I mean, I'm white, cops wouldn't shoot a white guy for wasting their time, right? But even if I'd come out of it alive, who likes to be laughed out of a police station by a bunch of cops?

No, I decided, I wouldn't take the note to the police. I'd just have to await further instructions.

11

Civility

It was Sunday morning at 10, time for one of my favorite TV shows, *Everybody's a Philosopher!* It's one of the longest-running programs on PBS, having debuted in 1965, and still with the original host, a Princeton philosophy professor, now emeritus and in his nineties. I started watching about 40 years ago, when the host had a shock of luxurious jet-black hair; over the years I've watched him go bald and turn gray. The premise of the show is that the week's interviewee is not some kind of expert or public figure, but rather a regular person, just like you or me or your next-door neighbor. The host, also the show's creator, calls it "an adventure in practical philosophy."

I turned the TV on and switched the channel to 13. The show's opening music came on, an abstract modern classical theme, the kind that was in vogue in the sixties. After the opening credits there's always a card with the topic of the day's program. This one said, "Has civility become extinct?" Then the scene shifted to the studio, in shadow.

As the lights came up on the host and guest, I was flabbergasted to recognize that the guest was the neighbor, *my* next-door neighbor. What was he doing on the show? I realize they'll take anyone, that's basically the whole premise of the thing, but *this* guy to talk about civility? What a laugh!

The host asked the guest, the neighbor, for his thoughts on civility, inspiring a veritable logorrhea of trite platitudes and dubious nostalgic claims about an idyllic past. What a tiresome bag of hot air, I thought. Then the host asked his guest for examples of the decline in civility, and that's when it became personal.

"Take my next-door neighbor," he said. "A walking advertisement for incivility. For instance, he blasts his music night and day, that weird jazz where everybody is honking and screeching."

"You mean free jazz?" the host asked.

"I wouldn't know," the neighbor said. "I only know it sounds like farm animals being slaughtered."

What a jerk. Besides being clueless about music, he was lying through his teeth. Night and day? There was one time, maybe 25 years ago, when he knocked on my door and without any opening pleasantries launched into a tirade of invective about my selfishness. I apologized, told him that I hadn't registered how loud it might sound beyond my walls because I had the water running to wash the dishes. I told him I'd turn it down, which I did. And he never came to complain again, all right, maybe two or three more times in all those years, so what's all this about night and day?

He continued. "And do you think he has any manners? Most of the time he doesn't even say hello, and when he does acknowledge me, in the lobby or the elevator, he never addresses me by name. We've been neighbors for over 30 years, and I don't think he even knows my name."

I do know his name, but I don't always remember it, sometimes I remember his first name but not his last, sometimes his last but not his first, so I just figure it's safer not to say his name. There are lots of people in the building whose names I don't know. What's the big deal?

"And I think the worst part is that sometimes when we run into each other I could swear he's looking right through me, as if

I'm not even there, like I'm some kind of ghost."

Is that true? I always try to make eye contact. So maybe I don't quite pull it off all the time.

"Well, I'm afraid we've run out of time," the host said. "I'd like to thank our guest…" I made a mental note of the neighbor's name.

"And thank you all for watching *Everybody's a Philosopher!* Be sure to tune in at the same time next week when my guest and I will try to answer that age-old question, 'Love thy neighbor as thyself?' And remember, this program is made possible by viewers like you."

12

Portrait

I was passing by the local elementary school, P.S. 321. It's considered one of the best public primary schools in the city. Real estate is at a premium in my immediate neighborhood because of it.

There were three little boys in front of the gate sitting at a little bridge table. "Hey mister, can you help us?" one of the boys asked.

"What do you need?"

"We're trying to raise money to buy a PlayStation. They're pretty expensive, you know, so we're doing portraits of people for a couple of bucks apiece," the same kid said.

"How are you doing so far?"

"Not great, so far we've made 18 bucks."

I was feeling generous, and I wasn't in a rush, so I said, "Sure, I'll let you do my portrait."

A different boy said, "Two dollars for one color, or five bucks for multiple."

I admired their initiative, so I said, "Multiple colors!"

It turned out the third kid, who hadn't said anything yet, was the artist. He took out a box of Crayola crayons and started making an outline in black on a sheet of cream-colored construction paper. I didn't want to make him self-conscious, so I didn't watch what he was doing.

As he continued to draw me, the other two would look over his work, sometimes point at something and whisper, sometimes suggest a different color to use in a certain spot. The whole operation took about three minutes.

"Wa-la," the kid who had first stopped me said as he handed me the drawing.

I was impressed and surprised. It was incredibly detailed and realistic. How had he done that in three minutes? He couldn't have been more than 10 or 11 years old.

"This is unbelievable," I said as I handed the artist a fin. "But how did you know what I looked like when I was your age?"

13

Transistor Radio

I found an old transistor radio on the street. It looked like the kinds I had when I was a kid. A transistor radio became an essential kid accessory when Beatlemania hit. One Saturday night back then I was going through the stations and I heard this guy doing a kind of stand-up act at a nightclub, only he wasn't telling jokes, he was telling stories, stories that were real and believable and weird and relatable and hilarious. I learned it was Jean Shepherd, broadcasting from his weekly gig at a club called The Limelight in Greenwich Village. It became a Saturday night ritual for me to listen to Shep with the radio under my pillow.

I often pick up books on the street, but electronics I generally pass by. This time, however, something, a pang of nostalgia, maybe, inspired me to take the radio. It was a Zenith.

I wondered if it would work. First I'd have to get a 9-volt battery. I wondered how easy it would be to find one. It used to be easy to get them at any newsstand, pharmacy, toy store, etc. I stopped into a small local pharmacy, but they didn't carry them. I struck paydirt at my next stop, a CVS.

I put the battery in the radio and turned it on. At first I heard static, then I started rolling the station dial. I heard a deejay. The voice sounded familiar. Then I heard the jingle. "Seventy-seven, WABC!" The top 40 station of my childhood. Then, "This is Dan Ingram bringing you number two, 'Do Wah Diddy Diddy,' by Manfred Mann."

That was really weird. They were playing an old broadcast from when I was a kid.

I changed the station. The news was on. "In today's top stories, the Nobel Prize committee has announced that this year's peace prize has been awarded to the Reverend Martin Luther King Jr."

Now weird things happen to me all the time, so I shouldn't have been surprised to have found a radio that only played broadcasts from my childhood, and I wasn't surprised, just annoyed. Yes, annoyed. Annoyed because it was such a cliché, finding a radio that broadcasts the past, like some *Twilight Zone* episode. I deserve better than that. I write stories about the weird things that happen to me, but I couldn't use this. Nobody would believe it. People would say I'm off my game, that I'm relying on hackneyed old plots. What a waste of my time. I was tempted to break the radio, I was so angry. I considered throwing it to the sidewalk and stomping it into oblivion. But why break a perfectly good old radio? So I decided to keep it, even if I couldn't milk it for a story.

That Saturday night I listened to Jean Shepherd with the radio under my pillow, even though at my age I could have played it as loud as I wanted.

14

The Picture of Peter Cherches

I was walking by the full-length mirror on the outside of my bathroom door when I did a double take. Instead of my mirror image, my face was a pastel portrait of me as a five-year-old; the rest of my body was as expected. I remembered that portrait. It was done in 1961, when my mother, my brother, and I spent the summer in The Catskills at The Tamarac Lodge.

One day a man came to The Tamarac to do portraits of interested guests. My mother had him do all three of us. The artist's name was Charles Biro, and he had a history, a serious one, actually. He had been a comic artist earlier in his career, most famous for *Daredevil Comics*. But his pastel portraits weren't in comic book style, they were realistic.

I hadn't seen that portrait in years. How did a pastel of my five-year-old head replace my sexagenarian head in the mirror?

I went into the bathroom to look in the other mirror, the one above the sink. Same thing. Normal torso, pastel head.

This was really freaking me out. I couldn't think of a plausible explanation. One mirror was bad enough, but two?

I'd have to leave my apartment and find an impartial mirror. I figured I'd go to the dry cleaner and tailor across the street. I knew they had a full-length mirror. As subterfuge, I brought a pair of pants for dry cleaning that I'd usually throw in a machine. I walked into the shop and put the pants on the counter. "Friday?" the Korean woman asked.

"Sure."

I took my receipt, and then I turned to look in the mirror. Same thing. Pastel head.

"Excuse me," I said to the woman.

"Yes?"

"Does my head look normal?"

She looked confused. "I don't remember seeing you before. Maybe you're not a regular customer," she said, "but you look fine."

"So nothing strange?"

"You look like American," she said.

Yeah, but did I look like an American of a certain age, or an American of a greatly reduced one? I didn't want to bother her anymore, so I called Allan Bealy, who lives a few blocks away. Allan, whom I've known for years, was editor of the downtown arts journal *Benzene* and the publisher of my first collection, *Condensed Book*. He answered. "Allan," I said, "by any chance are you free for me to stop by for a couple of minutes? There's something I need to ask you."

"Sure," he said. "I'm working on a new collage, but I can take a break. What's up?"

"I'll tell you when I get there."

When I got to Allan's apartment he asked me if I wanted anything to drink. "No thanks," I said. "Tell me, how old do I look?"

He thought for a second. "Well, you don't look your age!"

"How old do I look, five?"

"What? Of course not. Sometimes you act like you're five, but I'd say you could pass for 58, 59."

"So I don't look like a kid, and my head doesn't look like a pastel?"

"What are you talking about?"

I told him the whole story.

"That's nuts," he said. "Are you sure this isn't one of your stories?"

"I swear."

"Let's go into the bathroom and look in our mirror."

I followed him into the bathroom. We both looked in the mirror. I saw Allan, normal Allan, and me with the five-year-old pastel head. "What do you see?" I asked.

"You and me."

"And my head is normal?"

"As normal as it'll ever be."

"But I see the pastel head, the kid's head."

"Are you tripping?"

"Not for at least fifty years."

"Do you feel OK?"

"I felt fine until I started seeing the pastel head in every mirror!"

"You might want to see a shrink," he concluded.

I suspected he might be right, but maybe it was just a passing hallucination. I figured I'd wait. If nobody else noticed, then it wasn't such a big deal.

I went home and started reading a Val McDermid mystery. I got lost in the plot and forgot about my pastel-headed troubles for a while. Then I got up to make a cup of tea. I passed the full-length mirror on my way to the kitchen. I stopped and looked. Same thing.

This thing was throwing me for a loop. Was I really going crazy? I had to do something about it. I couldn't go on this way, always seeing that pastel head in my mirror. So I went to my desk, and from atop the hutch I picked up the little bronze Buddha I had bought at an antique shop in Thailand. I smashed the mirror to smithereens with it. I'd have to sweep the shards up, but first I had to take care of the bathroom mirror. I was pleasantly surprised when I saw that my head in that mirror was now normal, so I didn't have to smash it after all.

This was cause for celebration. I decided to go to the bar down the block for a drink. I'd take care of sweeping the shards when I got back.

When I got to the bar I took a stool and told the bartender, "Tanqueray on the rocks with a squeeze of lime, soda on the side."

"Get outta here," the bartender said. "You know we can't serve little boys."

15

The Tablecloth

When I was in my twenties I dated enough to have had my share of nightmare dates as well as weird ones. There's a difference between the two. With a nightmare date, the other party is the nightmare—maybe they're psychotic, paranoid, humorless, negative, or oversensitive. Maybe politically repugnant. A person you misjudged when you asked them out, who is annoying if not unbearable to be with, someone you can't wait to get away from. Weird dates, on the other hand, aren't always bad, sometimes they're amusing, but, well, weird. The person you're with isn't weird, circumstances become so.

One of the weirdest dates I remember took place in the late '70s, when I was working on my MFA in fiction writing. I had asked Connie, from the poetry program, out. Poets and fiction writers were always going out with each other, casually dating or forming relationships, much more so than within their own genres. You don't want to shit where you eat, or vice versa. You don't want to go on a date with someone you're going to see in a workshop the next day. You don't want to publicly critique the work of someone you're sleeping with.

We went to dinner at an Italian restaurant near the school, nothing fancy, but nice enough, especially on a student budget. Before dinner, we had attended a reading on campus by a visiting Estonian poet, big, burly, and bushy blond bearded, who read the original version of each poem followed by a translation, delivered in heavily accented English. He said, "Even if you don't understand Estonian, please listen for the music." We walked over to the restaurant afterwards.

Connie was laidback and low-key, and very smart, with a great sense of humor, the kind of woman I was often attracted to, a calming contrast to my own anxious nature. She was a WASP from somewhere in the Midwest (I knew where then, but the years have erased the location), a small city. She came from a financially comfortable family, somewhat more well off than my own solidly middle class Brooklyn Jewish one. We gossiped about our respective classmates and the politics of the program. I was pretty hungry, so when the waiter brought us some bread and butter I started right in on it. We ordered an antipasto to share, she chose a rigatoni special with eggplant and pancetta for her main, and I got the lasagna verde.

After we finished the antipasto, Connie excused herself and went to the bathroom. I amused myself with another piece of buttered bread.

After Connie had been away from the table for a while, it happened. Out of nowhere, a pigeon flew over my table and shat right on the tablecloth. How the pigeon got in the restaurant, I had no idea, but it was gone without a trace right after it had dropped its guano. The stain was disgusting, an irregular splotch with jagged edges, off-white with some streaks of yellow and little brown speckles. It reminded me of a crude attempt at a Clyfford Still painting.

Just then I saw Connie returning to the table. As she took her seat, I said, "You won't believe what happened while you were gone."

"What?"

"A pigeon flew in and took a shit on the tablecloth."

"What?"

I pointed at the stain on the tablecloth. "Look!"

She looked. "Is that pigeon poop?"

Poop? You know she wasn't a native New Yorker. "Of course it is! It's from the pigeon that flew over the table."

She looked again. "I guess from a certain angle it kinda looks like pigeon poop."

"Kinda? Of course it's pigeon shit. Why would I lie about such a thing?"

"Oh, I have no reason to doubt you if that's what you say it is."

"I'm gonna call the waiter over." I caught the waiter's eye and called him over. "Excuse me."

The waiter came over. "Yes, sir, what can I do for you?"

I told him the story. "I don't know how it got in here, but a pigeon flew over the table and shat right on the tablecloth." I pointed at the stain.

He looked. "I don't think that's pigeon droppings," he said. "It looks to me like a shmear of butter with some crumbs from the bread crust mixed in."

Shmear? What kind of Italian waiter says shmear? All right, it *was* New York, after all.

"That's no bread and butter! That's pigeon shit!" I replied.

Just then a guy from another table yelled over at us, "Excuse me, can you keep it down? We can't enjoy our chicken cacciatore while you're yelling about pigeon shit!"

I didn't realize how loud my voice had gotten, but I couldn't argue with him. The guano stain was making me lose my own appetite. "Sorry," I yelled back.

Connie also made contact with the other table. "How's the chicken, by the way? I was thinking of ordering it, but I went for the rigatoni special instead."

"It's great," the woman at the other table answered.

"Getting back to the problem at hand," I said to the waiter, "would it be possible to change the tablecloth?"

"Let me talk to the manager," he said, and walked away.

"Let's hope the manager can make things right," I told Connie.

"I've got my fingers crossed," she said.

We sat in silence, and soon a big guy in a black suit came over. "Your waiter, Tony, tells me there's a problem."

"Yes, as I told Tony, a pigeon flew in and took a dump on the tablecloth, so we'd like to get it changed."

He looked at the tablecloth. "That looks like a food stain to me."

"I saw the pigeon with my own eyes," I said.

"Did *you* also see the pigeon?" he asked Connie.

"No, I was in the bathroom when it happened."

"Did *anybody* else see it?"

"How should I know?" I replied.

The manager called over to another table near ours. "Excuse me, sorry to bother you. Did you folks see a pigeon flying around the room a few minutes ago?"

"No," the couple said in unison.

"Well," I said, "it was very quick. But all I'm asking is if we can get a new tablecloth."

The manager said, "Normally I'd be happy to accommodate you, but it's the end of service, and all the other tablecloths are dirty and ready for the laundry."

"I'd settle for one of those," I said. "A marinara stain is preferable to pigeon shit."

A guy at yet another table called over. "Can you watch your language? We got kids here."

The manager said, "Sorry, we can't do that. It's against the health regulations. We'd get a citation."

"But it's not against the regulations to let people eat at a table full of pigeon, um, droppings?"

"We'll just have to agree to disagree about the nature of the stain," he said, and walked away.

I flushed red. "The nerve of that guy!" I said to Connie.

"Let's just try to ignore it," she said, calmly.

I considered arguing with her about it. As much as I liked calm, laidback women, I also liked women who could give me a run for my money in an argument. But I didn't think Connie had the makings of a sparring partner, so I held my peace.

Just then the waiter arrived with our entrees. "Rigatoni for the lady," he said as he put the plate in front of Connie. "And lasagna verde al forno for the gentleman. Is there anything else I can get you?"

I looked at Connie, who shook her head. I bit my tongue and said, "No thanks."

"Buon appetito," he said, and walked away.

Connie started eating her rigatoni while I looked at my lasagna. "This is really good," she said.

I picked at the lasagna, took a few small bites, but I just couldn't eat it when push came to shove. The pigeon shit had made me lose my appetite.

We talked about literary awards and conferences and retreats while she enjoyed her rigatoni and I tried to keep my eyes off both the lasagna and the stain.

When Connie's plate was clean, the waiter returned. He saw my barely touched lasagna.

"Was everything all right?" he asked, staring straight at me.

"Oh, just fine," I said, forcing myself to take a diplomatic approach. "I guess I just wasn't that hungry."

"Would you like us to pack it up for you to take home?"

"I don't think..."

"Sure, why not," Connie said, looking at me. "No point in letting it go to waste."

"Sure," I said, resigned.

"Can I get you any dessert or coffee?" Tony asked.

I looked at Connie. "Would you like coffee or dessert," I asked her lugubriously, hoping she'd get the message and say no.

"I don't think so," she said, to my great relief.

"Then I'll get this packed up for you and be right back with the check," he said, and took my lasagna plate with him. He returned a few minutes later with the check and the bag.

I picked up the check. "I'll take care of this," I said. Now, mind you, this was a time when a check could become a bone of sexual politics contention, it no longer being safe to assume that the man should pay for dinner.

"Oh no," she said, "I thought we were going Dutch."

"You can get the next one," I said, and she didn't protest any further.

We left the restaurant and I walked Connie back to her building, not far from the restaurant. As we were parting she gave me a peck on the cheek. "Well, thanks for a really interesting evening!"

"That it was," I said, and headed toward the subway a few blocks away, with my doggie bag.

In the end, I never ate that leftover lasagna. For two days I'd take it out of the fridge to heat up, look at it, and all I could think about was that pigeon shit stain on the tablecloth, so I threw it out on day three.

I never had a second date with Connie, neither of us ever

brought it up, but we continued our cordial chats whenever we'd meet in the student lounge. We lost touch after we got our degrees, but I followed her career. She was one of the real success stories of the program. Connie's now a distinguished full professor at a big Midwestern university, has won some of the most prestigious poetry awards and been nominated for most of the others. According to her biography, her poems have been translated into more than 15 languages. Her daughter Katie made last year's "30 Novelists Under 40" list.

The Italian restaurant finally closed about five years ago, after a successful 70-year run.

As for me, never again has a pigeon taken a crap on my dinner table. On the right shoulder of my Harris tweed overcoat, yes.

16

Customer Service

I called the utility company to discuss a dispute with my bill. After an interminable wait on hold, where all the music seemed to be sung by Michael McDonald, a customer service rep finally picked up. "Hello, my name is Ricky. How can I help you today?"

There was something familiar about that voice, but I couldn't place it.

I told him there was a problem with my bill and gave him my account info.

"All right," he said, "give me a moment while I pull up your record."

That voice. I figured out who it sounded like: the neighbor. But I was pretty sure the neighbor didn't work for the utility company, and even if he did, what are the odds that I'd get him?

"Sorry for the delay, it'll only be a little longer," the customer service rep said. Then, as if he had read my mind, he added, "Boy, it's really hot here in Manila today. How's the weather where you are?"

"Oh, fine," I said. "I don't think Brooklyn ever gets as hot as Manila."

"All right, Mr. Cherches, I have your record in front of me. How can I help you?"

I explained the problem with the bill. It clearly was an error. It was more than double my previous bill, and my usage pattern hadn't changed at all.

"All right, let me review that," he said. "Please allow me to put you on hold."

"All right," I said, and was greeted in return by Bachman-Turner Overdrive.

He came back on the line. "Sorry for the delay. I have reviewed your bill and determined there is no problem."

"What do you mean no problem?"

"Based on the cost per unit, the total is correct for your usage during this billing period."

"That's the problem," I said. "The usage number can't be correct."

"Oh, I can assure you, sir, that number is correct. The usage number is always correct."

"What, I'm just supposed to believe you?"

"I have worked for this company for many years, sir. I am in a position to know."

"Well this is one thing you don't know. So what are my options?"

"You have no options, sir."

That arrogant little twit. And "hot in Manila" notwithstanding, that really sounded like the neighbor. Whoever it was, I figured he wasn't the final authority, so I said, "Is there someone I can speak to who has more authority?" I realize I was beginning to sound like a Karen, but I used to work in customer service, and I know there's always a superior with more authority.

"There is nobody with more authority," he said.

I was livid. But what could I do, at least on this phone call, at this time? "All right," I said, "I'll deal with this some other way."

"There is no other way," he said.

"Well, thanks for your help anyway," I said.

"You're very welcome. Is there anything else I can help you

with today?"

"Hell no!"

"Thank you. You will shortly be sent a brief survey about your experience with us today. We hope you'll take the time to provide your feedback." Then the call was dropped.

About a minute later, my doorbell rang. "Who is it?" I asked.

"Your neighbor." I opened the door. The neighbor handed me a large manila envelope. "Here's your survey," he said. "Please return it by 3 p.m. today." Then he added, "Magandang araw!"

17

The New Guest

My mail-order android arrived this afternoon. I bought one of the new energy-efficient models to replace my old legacy golem. I like its clean Scandinavian lines, so I decided to call it Lars. I plugged Lars in to charge, and within an hour its pupils had changed from red to green. I've sat Lars down in the guest chair, formerly inhabited by the golem, Zalman. I left Zalman in front of my building and taped a sign to its chest that reads: Works. Please take.

18

Fred, Rick, and Me

I got rid of my land line years ago, but I wanted to keep my old phone number, so I ported it to a VoIP account and set calls to go directly to voicemail. That way I could still use it for businesses I don't want to give my cell number to, and also, since I'd had that number for so many years, in case anybody from the past wanted to get in touch with me. When somebody leaves a voicemail, I get an email with an MP3 of the message attached.

The other day I was going through my inbox and saw an email from my VoIP provider with the subject: New Voicemail. I opened the message and downloaded the audio file. I listened to the message. "Hi Peter, you probably don't remember me. My name is Rick Stahl, and we knew each other in college. You might remember me as Fred." I did remember him, vaguely. "Anyway," the voice said, "I'm back in Brooklyn for a few days, and I'm wondering if we could meet for a coffee or something." He left his number.

I was surprised to get his call. It's not like we were ever close or anything. I remember him as a nice guy, an English major, who was in several of the same classes as me. And I remembered his transition from Fred to Rick.

Fred was a soft-spoken, short, slight-of-build guy who wore glasses with thick black frames, Buddy Holly-style, before they became ironically hip again. I ran into him once again after college, and he was completely transformed. He no longer wore glasses, so I figured contacts. He was tanned, and no longer had the body of a 98-pound weakling; he was wearing a tight black T-shirt; clearly he'd been working out. There was a gold chain around his neck. He seemed much more self-confident.

"Fred!" I said. "How are you doing? You're looking great."

"I'm not Fred anymore, it's Rick," he said.

"Oh?" I asked.

"It was my shrink's idea. I was complaining about not meeting women, wanting a relationship, and he told me my problem was I had the self-image of a Fred. He suggested I change my name and my attitude, and it actually worked. I'm happy, I'm taking care of myself, and I have a great girlfriend."

I congratulated him, gave him a very brief account of what I was up to and we parted. I was actually hoping he'd show me a photo of his girlfriend, but he never offered. That must have been at least 40 years ago, and I'd never seen or heard from him again.

Now, out of the blue, I get this call.

Well, why not, I thought. He was a nice guy, and I enjoy social intercourse in controlled environments with a reasonable mutual assumption of time limitations. So I called the number he left.

"Hello?"

"Rick?"

"Yes."

"This is Pete Cherches, returning your call. Peter."

I had changed my name too, in a small way. I kept Peter Cherches as my nom de plume, but starting at around age 25, actually not long after I had last seen Rick, I decided I liked the breezy informality of Pete in my everyday life. It had no effect on my physique or my love life, at least not that I was aware of.

We agreed to meet by the college, for old times' sake, at The Campus Coffee Shop, a couple of days later.

I got to the coffee shop first. I had looked around and didn't see anybody the right age to be Rick. A few minutes later a bald, chubby sexagenarian walked in. Definitely not Rick, I thought, but then he came up to my table and said, "Peter?" And I thought, oh yes, Rick's face is buried in there somewhere.

I stood up and shook his hand. "Nice to see you again."

When I knew him he looked kind of like Sal Mineo. But the guy I was looking at now was more of the Jackie Coogan, Joe Besser, or Don Rickles type.

"You haven't changed, Peter. I'd recognize you anywhere," he said, as he took a seat.

"You can call me Pete," I said, without commenting on his looks.

"Aha! So you did it too! Changes everything, right?"

"What do you mean?"

"The name change."

"Oh," I said. "I just like the informality of Pete."

"I see."

I said, "I was surprised to hear from you after all these years."

"Well, when you get to be our age those old friendships start to take on a new importance." I didn't mention that we were never really friends. "So I figured as long as I was coming for a visit we ought to catch up."

"Glad you did."

"Remember when I changed my name to Rick?" he said.

"Sure, and everything changed for the better."

"For a while, maybe, but look at me now."

I hadn't stopped looking.

"Well, we're all getting older."

"Yeah, but in my case it happened sooner than later, and it was all Chanterelle's fault."

"Chanterelle?"

"Yeah, my girlfriend. I couldn't believe my luck. She looked like a freakin' model. And wild in bed like you wouldn't believe." I was starting to envy his former self.

"So what went wrong?"

"She met another guy."

"Well, these things happen. They sting for a while, but we have to move on."

"I wish that were so in my case, but it was who she left me for that irked the hell out of me."

"Someone I know?"

"Yeah, Arnold Markowitz. Remember him from college?"

I certainly did, though the only memorable thing about him was what an out-of-shape schlub he was for someone who wasn't even old enough to drink. He was prematurely bald with greasy, stringy hair on the sides, had a body best described as roly-poly, a whiny voice, and perennially bad breath. I couldn't remember anything else about him. Was he smart? What were his interests?

"I do," I said.

"I couldn't believe it. Here I was, all buff and tanned, a regular Adonis if you don't mind my saying, and there she was leaving me for a loser like that. I was so angry and depressed that I started letting myself go to pot. Binge eating, couch potato, you name it. Then, after a while, when I was fat and out of shape, I realized, wait a minute, maybe I had become the type she really went for. So I called her. I said to her, 'Chanterelle, can we give it another go? I've changed. I know you think I was unbearably vain and self-centered, but that's all over. I've turned over a new leaf.' And you know what she said? She said, 'I've told you, Rick, it's all over. Arnold and I are very happy together.' Then I said, 'Forget about Rick. Rick is dead. Call me Fred. Can't we at least get together for a coffee or something?' And she said, 'I don't think that's a good idea, Rick, I mean Fred.'"

"So you never saw her again?"

"Nope. Never on purpose, never by accident. But I did see Arnold once, on the street. I almost didn't recognize him. He had lost weight, gotten into shape, and was wearing a tight shirt that showed off his pecs, with the top three or four buttons open, revealing a hairy chest. I mean Wolf Man hairy. He had shaved his head, and it looked kinda good on him. When he spoke his breath smelled of violet mints. 'Man,' I said, 'you're looking great. When did all this happen, the new you, I mean?' And he said, 'A few years after college. I was tired of being someone everybody thought of as an unattractive lump, so I took the bull by the horns and started working out, and everything just kind of fell into place. And I mean big time. I met this great girl. Smart, sexy, beautiful, amazing in bed, sometimes almost more than I can handle, but not quite—I couldn't believe my luck. You'd like her.'"

"Bummer," I said.

"Yeah, and then I said to him, 'What about your name?' And he said, 'What about my name?' So I said, 'I don't know, do you think Arnold goes with your new look? Not even Arnie?'"

"And what did he say?"

"He said, 'I like Arnold. Arnold is my name. It's who I am. I hate it when people call me Arnie.'"

After that Rick and I made small talk, nothing worth recounting. About a half hour later we shook hands again and parted. When I got home I plopped down in my easy chair and thought about how thankful I was that *I* had never really considered making such a drastic change, though I was glad I had grown more comfortably into whatever, whoever, I, Pete or Peter, Pete and Peter, was.

19

Help!

The guy sitting down on the sidewalk, leaning against the side of a building, had a sign that said "HELP!" I pulled a single out of my wallet and tried to hand it to him. He slapped my hand away. "I don't need your filthy lucre," he barked at me.

"But your sign said 'HELP!' I thought you needed money."

"Don't need no money," he grumbled. "I need help."

"What kind of help?"

"You name it," he said. "Help tying my shoes in the morning; damn arthritis. Help balancing my checkbook. Help getting it up, and then help achieving an orgasm. Help navigating the bureaucracy. Help finding my daughter who hasn't been in touch in 27 years. Help operating the VCR; I've had the damn thing for 40 years and I still don't know how to work it. Help with my anger issues. Help reaching the items on the top shelf. Help making sense of this mad world we live in."

"Sorry," I said, "can't help." Then I went looking for a real panhandler as long as I still had the buck in my hand.

20

Mesmerized

I couldn't stop looking at it. I was mesmerized. It really had a hold on me. So much, in fact, that I sang it as I stared, the Smokey Robinson song.

It had a special kind of beauty, the kind where one single strategically placed imperfection makes all the difference in the world.

It was mysterious, an enigma, and that only made me more obsessed with it. I sensed there were vast secrets to be mined if I could only find the key.

I had lost all sense of proportion. I was ready to do anything, to up-end my life, give up everything I'd previously held sacred. My principles, my dreams, they were all on the table. Even suicide. Yes, I was prepared to die, if that's what was required of me.

As I contemplated suicide, the waitress came by and asked, "Are you still workin' on that, hon?"

21

A Tip

"Excuse me," I said, "you dropped something."

The woman turned around. "I didn't drop anything," she said angrily, in an accent I couldn't place.

"Right there," I said, pointing down at the sidewalk.

"Oh, my coin purse! Thank you." She picked it up. She took a quarter out to give me a tip.

"Oh, please, no, it was my pleasure."

"What, my money's not good enough for you?"

"Of course it's good enough for me, but I don't need it."

"What makes you so special that you don't need a quarter?"

"Nothing. Nothing makes me special. So give me the quarter."

She gave me the quarter. I looked at it. It wasn't a quarter. It was foreign currency from I didn't know where.

"This isn't a quarter," I said, "it's a foreign coin."

"Well, aren't you hoity-toity!"

"I was just letting you know, in case you needed it."

"How dare you insult me! Do I look like I need a measly schmonski?"

"Did you say schmonski?"

"Yes, why?"

"I've been looking for a schmonski for years, for my collection! I thought they were discontinued."

"This is a novy schmonski. The government started issuing them last year because the people were nostalgic for the schmonski."

"What's a schmonski worth these days?" I asked.

"About a quarter."

22

Whose Dream?

I'm huddled in a crowd. I smell sweat all around me, I smell fear, the acrid scent of adrenaline. I'm dreaming in black and white; that's odd, I always dream in color. The time is not now, it's another time, early 1940s, I'd say. I'm wearing a ragged old overcoat, my face all stubble. The men, many are stone-faced, staring into a void, others heads hung, some quietly weeping, some muttering prayers. Women are sobbing, wailing, holding children close to their breasts. A couple of little boys are rough-housing off to the side, seemingly unaware of what's going on.

We're standing by a railway siding. I see boxcars, open, empty, nothing inside, just space. I realize we're in Nazi Germany, or perhaps occupied Poland, and I'm waiting for transport to a death camp.

The kommandant—I assume that's what you call the uni-formed personage barking orders—looks disturbingly familiar. I realize why: it's the neighbor. "Schnell! Schnell!" the neighbor keeps yelling.

That prick, I think, he's everywhere.

Then he does something odd—he puts his hand to his face and starts tugging at his skin. The skin on his face starts bunch-ing up as he pulls. It comes off. It was a mask. It's not the neigh-bor's face underneath, it's mine, clean shaven.

He goose steps his way over to me. "Achtung!" he barks. I stand at attention. He puts his hand to my face, does the same thing, pulls a mask off, and shows me my real face in a mirror.

I'm not me, I'm him.

But I (the dreamer, that is) am still identifying with the trembling, quaking shadow of a man destined for the cattle car, despite the change of face. The one with my face, the robust, well-fed Nazi, is a pretender, a phony, a fraud.

Is the neighbor sending me to my death, or is it the other way around?

I've always heard that you can't die in your own dream, but whose dream is this?

23

Vanities

"Vanity of vanities, all is vanity," I told the mirror above my vanity.

"I'm above vanity," the mirror above the vanity replied.

"Nobody is above vanity."

"I am nobody and I am anybody," said the mirror.

"Are you anybody now?"

"I am you."

"Am I above vanity?"

"You are at vanity's level, but I reflect your potential to rise above it."

I was pleased with that answer, so I walked away.

"Wait," the mirror yelled. "How can I help you if you walk away?"

24

Well-Beyond Impossible

The diner was having a special promotion for what I assumed to be a new vegan hamburger. It was called the Well-Beyond Impossible Burger. For $8.95 it included a strip of Untenable bacon, a slice of Inconceivable cheese, and a side of Prohibited fries. I actually wanted a real hamburger, but with the way prices have gotten out of control, I figured I might as well try the substitute while it was so cheap.

I didn't really have high hopes, but I did have certain expectations.

The waitress brought a plate that looked rather sparse. On closer inspection, I noticed there were no fries, and while there was a hamburger bun, there was nothing on it.

I called the waitress back. "I think there's been a mixup," I said. "I ordered the Well-Beyond Impossible Burger special."

"Yes," she said, "that's what I brought you."

"It was supposed to come with fries."

"No," she said, "the fries are Prohibited. We're not allowed to serve them."

"Then why do you list them on the menu?"

"It's part of the combination," she said. "People want a well-rounded meal."

"And what about this so-called burger? All I see is a bun."

"The burger is Well-Beyond Impossible, and we haven't the slightest idea how to make one. Same with the cheese. It's so Inconceivable, our suppliers just laughed at us when we brought it up. And the bacon is simply Untenable. We won't stand for it. So, as you can see, our only option is to serve a plain bun."

"Can I at least have some butter?"

"We don't have any butter," she said, "but I can bring you some I Can't Believe It's Not Butter."

"All right," I said with a sigh, resigned. The waitress left my table, and a minute or so later she returned with one of those little bowls that diners use to hold environmentally unfriendly single servings of butter and jelly.

"Hey," I said to the waitress, "this bowl is empty!"

"I know," she said. "Can you believe it?"

25

Clowns

Two clowns were sitting at the booth across from my table at the diner. I didn't think there was a circus in town, so I figured maybe they were booked for a kid's birthday party or something. I know clowns have a reputation for being gruff and nasty when they're off duty, but I figured I'd try to chat them up. I walked over to their booth.

"Excuse me, fellas," I said, "I couldn't help noticing your costumes, and I was wondering where you were performing."

They seemed confused. One of them said, "Performing?"

"Yeah," I said. "Is there a circus in town, or are you doing a private party."

They still looked confused.

"We're having lunch," the other clown said.

"Yeah, I can see that. Are you coming from the gig or preparing?"

"What gig?" the second clown asked.

"The clown gig."

They were silent.

"I was just curious," I said. "I didn't mean to interrupt your lunch. I'll just leave you alone." I was about to walk away when the first clown spoke again.

"You seem to think we're performers," he said. "Whatever gave you that impression?"

"The clown costumes!"

"Costumes?" the other said. "These are our clothes."

"But aren't you clowns?"

"Of course we're clowns," the second one said. "But we're not performers."

"I don't understand. If you're not performers, what do you do?"

"I'm a dentist," the first one said, "and he's an accountant."

"Then why are you dressed like clowns?"

They both looked at me like I was from another planet.

"Because we're clowns!" they responded in unison.

26

The Cherches Gallery

For several days I'd had an earworm of *The Addams Family* theme song, especially "Their house is a museum / When people come to see 'em." Then it happened to me.

It literally happened overnight. And I mean "literally" in the original sense of the word. I woke up one morning and discovered that my studio apartment had been transformed into a museum. Whoever did the work must have been incredibly quick and quiet.

My apartment is rather small for a museum, so maybe "gallery" would be the more appropriate term. The collection was very eclectic. There were Pre-Columbian artifacts, shrunken heads, a tea kettle with a sleek Danish design, a display of 1950s jazz album covers by Andy Warhol and *Mad* magazine's Don Martin, and a Vermeer hanging on the wall. That seemed like a major coup for such a small museum, a Vermeer.

Then I noticed I was not alone. There were visitors admiring the collection. I heard a man, apparently a tour guide, speaking to a small group.

"So we are now in the famous Cherches Gallery. Thanks to the generosity of writer Peter Cherches, we have this little jewel box of a museum, perhaps the most unique museum in Brooklyn." (I long ago accepted the inevitability of the phrase "most unique.") "And it's close enough to The Brooklyn Museum of Art that one can easily visit both in the same day. Just make sure to plan your visit around the Brooklyn Museum's closing days, which are

Mondays and Tuesdays. The Cherches Gallery, on the other hand, is open 24/7."

24/7? Does that mean I'll have to put up with strangers in my apartment night and day, day in and day out? I didn't remember ever authorizing such a thing.

The guide pointed at the Vermeer. "This, of course, is the gallery's most prized painting, by Johannes Vermeer, and it's worth a quick look, but the real heart of the collection is over here." He pointed at me sitting up in my bed.

"Yes, Peter Cherches himself! Cherches has long been interested in making his persona the center of his own work, so he decided that he should also be the pièce de résistance of his own gallery. His corpus, as it were." I heard sighs of admiration. "Please have a look."

A group of five tourists, one an old-timer with a camera around his neck, gathered around my bed and gawked at me.

"He looks older than in the photos," one of them said. Of course I looked older than in my photos. I am older than in my photos.

Then a middle-aged woman, somewhat zaftig, in jeans and sensible shoes, reached out and touched me.

"Hey," I yelled out, "this is a gallery, not a petting zoo!"

"Oh, shorry, shorry," the woman apologized in a Dutch accent.

27

The Neighbor Asks a Question

One day in the elevator the neighbor asked me something surprising. It was surprising enough that he even asked me something, since he often stares at his shoes and ignores me if we happen to be sharing the elevator. He asked me, "You know Judy Lieberman, don't you?"

The only Judy Lieberman I could remember was a grade-school classmate, and all I could remember about her was the Valentine's Day card. It was our teacher's idea, and I can't imagine such a scheme would fly today. We would pick a name at random from a box and send a Valentine's Day card to that person. The boys picked from a box of girls' names, and vice versa. So each boy would send a card to one girl classmate, and a different girl, in my case Judy Lieberman, would send one to a boy. I suppose a boy and a girl could have drawn each other, but I don't know what the odds would be, given about 15 names of each gender. I can't remember who I sent mine to, but I'm pretty sure it wasn't Judy Lieberman, and I'm positive it wasn't Susan Klugman, my arch-enemy from spelling bee—that I'd have remembered. I do remember Judy Lieberman's Valentine's Day card. It had a drawing of a dachshund and it said "I long to be your Valentine." Why was the neighbor asking me about Judy Lieberman?

"Well," I said, "I went to school with a girl named Judy Lieberman, but I haven't thought about her in over fifty years."

"As I thought," he said.

As he thought? Why did he think anything about me and Judy Lieberman? How did he even know about her? As far as I know, he's not from the old neighborhood.

"Did you go to P.S. 217?" I asked him.

"No."

"Did you know Judy Lieberman?"

"No."

"Then why did you ask me if I knew her?"

"Just checking," he replied as the door opened to the lobby.

28

Human Kindness

As I was taking a walk around the perimeter of Prospect Park, a voice called out from behind. "Excuse me."

I turned around and looked. It was a middle-aged man in a seersucker suit.

"Yes?"

"Oh, thanks for stopping," he said. "I have this terrible itch on my back. Can you scratch it?"

That's never happened to me before, a total stranger asking me to scratch his back. I'm a naturally cautious New Yorker. Was this some kind of setup?

"I'm not sure about that," I said. "I don't know you."

"Phil Grossman," he said.

"Pete Cherches," I said.

"So now we know each other. So can you scratch my back?"

"I'm not big on physical contact outside of certain proscribed realms," I replied, "and this isn't one of them."

"Come on, be a pal, be a mensch, be a good Samaritan."

So now he was trying to guilt me.

"Listen," I said, "I wish you luck, but I'm not the guy for the job."

"There's nobody else around. If I were lying in the street bleeding and moaning for help would you pass me by?"

"But you're not lying in the street bleeding and moaning for help; you have an itchy back."

"Does that make me any less worthy of a little human kindness?"

"Why don't you do what I do when I have an itchy back? Find some kind of pole, preferably with angles, that you can rub up against."

"You know as well as I do that never works as well as the human touch."

I couldn't deny he was right. And it wasn't so easy to find angles. Should I help him?

"All right," I said, "but just a short scratch."

He took his jacket off. There was a big patch of sweat on the back of his shirt. He wanted me to scratch his sweaty shirt? That was more than I had bargained for.

"Your shirt's really sweaty," I said.

"Duh! It's only like 92 degrees with a real feel of 101."

"Sorry, I really don't think I can touch that sweaty shirt."

He didn't say anything, he just started taking his shirt off.

"Whoa! I didn't mean I was going to scratch your sweaty bare back."

"Make up your mind!"

"Look," I said, "an itchy back is not the end of the world."

"That's easy for you to say."

"It *is* easy. I get itchy backs all the time. They're annoying and uncomfortable, but even if it's not the ideal solution you can always use a pole."

"All right, all right, be selfish. I'll just have to take care of this my own way."

"Good luck," I said. "I really mean it."

The next thing I knew the shirtless Grossman was lying on the sidewalk, violently rubbing his back against the hot concrete. He started moaning. Then he turned over on his stomach. I saw that his back was all red, and blood was coming from the abrasions. "Oh, oh, help me somebody," he moaned.

I really hate people who won't take no for an answer.

29

A New Suit

I wanted something to jazz up my look. I wanted people to say, "That guy rocks." Something modern, but with a classic cut. Perhaps a suit in three or four different shades of blue. I went to my old tailor on Orchard Street. And I mean old. When I started seeing him back in the late '70s he seemed to already be in his late 60s. This was when there were still lots of Jewish tailors of a certain age on Orchard Street. Now the street is populated with hip bars and restaurants, no longer primarily the old Jewish businesses of all sorts run by old Jewish men in various stages of observant—businesses like tefillin-checking joints and matzoh outlets, not to mention the more secular garment and bedding shops.

My tailor's name is Moe. Moe Rabinowitz. He has the classic Lower East Side old-Jew accent, though I long ago discovered his dirty secret: one time, when he hadn't noticed that I had entered the shop, I overheard him on the phone, and he was speaking perfectly unaccented American news-anchor English. When he got off the phone he said to me, "So, mine friend, vat is it I can do for you today?" I didn't let on that I knew the truth. He clearly felt he needed to keep the charade up for the sake of his business, for his customers' expectations.

This time, so many years later, I was surprised at how spry he was for someone who was certainly a centenarian, if not—what would one call it, a centedecanarian? "Vell, mine friend, I heffen't seen you in a dog's age at least."

"Well, you know," I said, "business casual and all. But now that I'm retired I'd like to wear a suit again." This desire of mine must have had some deep atavistic origin, perhaps my memory of all the retired old Jewish men in my old Brooklyn neighborhood who continued to wear suits and hats, even in the dog days of summer.

"Any particular color?" Moe asked.

"That's the thing," I said. "I would like a blue suit, but I would like it to have multiple shades of blue."

"This maybe we can do," he said, "if you don't mind plaid, that is." I nodded. "Foist, let me check your inseam," he said. He got out his tape measure and I spread my legs. He started at the top of my shoes and brought the measure up to my crotch. Then he surprised me by squeezing my balls. "Cough!" he said.

"Cough?" I asked.

"Yes," Moe said, "I heff to check for a hoinia!"

Why would a tailor have to check for a hernia? "Why do you have to check for a hernia?" I asked. "I just want a new suit."

"It's mine Hippocratic oat!" he said.

"Hippocratic oath? For a tailor?" I asked.

"Oh, I just keep this shop for old times' sake. Didn't you know? I got mine M.D. beck in the Reagan era. So now I do a little general practice, a little urology, and a bisl tailoring for the old customers."

I coughed. "Poifect," he said. Then he went in the back of the shop and returned a few minutes later with a really nice suit, plaid with multiple shades of blue, just what I was looking for. I tried it on and it was a perfect fit. "I'll take it," I said.

"Mazel tov. You vant I should put it on a hanger or in a box."

"Oh, I'll just wear it, if that's all right. You can throw my old stuff out."

Now I was all set to start my retirement in style.

30

The Package

It was a Wednesday in late November. There was a package for me in the mail. Who could it be from? I never receive packages. The only mail I receive is bills and junk mail. It was a very small package. I wondered what was in it. I tore the brown craft paper with the postage and my address off. There was no return address. The small box was gift wrapped, nondescript gift wrap. It didn't appear to be aimed at any particular occasion. It was the size of a box you'd find a watch in, or a bracelet. I removed the gift wrap. The box was red, red silk on stiff board. There was no card. I opened the box. Inside was not an item of jewelry, it was a Thanksgiving dinner, a piping hot miniature turkey with crispy skin, roasted sweet potatoes, stuffing, green beans, and cranberry sauce. It smelled great. Somebody must have gone to a lot of trouble to make such a perfect miniature Thanksgiving dinner. I figured I should try it before it got cold. So I ate the turkey in one bite, bones and all. It was, after all, considerably smaller than a lark. It was delicious, but hardly filling. Could this be an advertising scheme? Would I get a call later to ask me how I liked the sample, and then take my order for a full Thanksgiving dinner when I raved about how great the teaser was? But no, that wasn't it, no call ever came. So on Thanksgiving day I ate the leftover stuffing, sweet potatoes, green beans, and cranberry sauce.

31

Collected Stories

The thud woke me. My first thought was that something must have fallen to the floor from above. What time is it? 4:35. I got out of bed and turned on the light. It was right there on the kilim I bought in Istanbul nine years ago, a book, a book I hadn't yet read, from the top of a precarious pile atop the bookcase. I found the book on the stoop of one of the brownstones in my neighborhood. This was a book of short stories. I remembered that I'd been intrigued by the description on the back. The writer was unfamiliar to me, an unknown quantity. I took it on faith. That's easy with free books.

I picked the book up, to put on the nightstand to be "reshelved" in the morning. Then I started leafing through it. I should have gone right back to bed, but something I noticed inside the book demanded my immediate attention. I sat down in my easy chair and turned on the reading lamp. It was weird, and it was infuriating. All the stories in this book appeared to be rewritings of my own short fiction. Details were changed, sure, but at their core they were my stories. For instance, my "Mr. Deadman" series, the adventures of a corpse who won't be kept down, was now titled "The Many Lives (and Deaths) of Cristo Thanatos." And, in this scurrilous pile of plagiarism, "Mr. Cherches Goes to Mars" had become "Mr. Thanatos Goes to Venus." Instead of Martian pot roast, Mr. Thanatos was trying to find the secret Venusian recipe for moussaka. Then I remembered what had intrigued me about the book. I looked at the back cover and read the description. "In what *The Wall Street Journal* has called 'a mind-bending conceptual tour de force,' Cristo Thanatos has reimagined the obscure short stories of an almost completely unknown writer. As *The New Republic* put it so succinctly, 'Thanatos is a Borges for our time.'" So what, now I'm the butt of some big conceptual joke? The nerve of that Thanatos character! I should have gone back to bed, but I kept reading. After a while I could feel myself nodding off.

I woke up in bed and looked at the alarm clock. 7:35. I must have fallen asleep in the chair and gotten up at some point to get back in bed. Then I noticed the book on the kilim, exactly where I had picked it up three hours earlier. I realized what surely must have happened. I probably opened my eyes, noticed a book on the floor, then went right back to sleep, having decided to deal with it in the morning. Then I had that silly dream about how my work had been plagiarized. I laughed at the ridiculousness of it all. Cristo Thanatos! Doesn't that mean Christ Death?

I got out of bed and bent down to pick up the book. I looked at the title. *The Collected Stories of Cristo Thanatos.*

32

Christian Commercial

I was watching TV late one night, around 2 a.m. A commercial for a Christian ministry came on. The wee hours is prime time for evangelical advertising. "When God knocks on your door, will you open it?" the voiceover asked.

Just then there was a knock on my door.

I ran to the door and looked through the peephole.

It was the neighbor.

"What is it?" I asked, loud enough to be heard through the closed door.

"CAN YOU TURN THAT DAMN THING DOWN?" he yelled back, at the top of his voice.

33

Closed Indefinitely

So, after three transfers, one more than expected, due to a rerouting caused by some kind of incident, no further details forthcoming, on one of the main thoroughfares, necessitating I walk three blocks out of my way to catch the alternate bus that would get me to my destination in the shortest amount of time, what do I discover but that the place is no longer there. I don't mean closed, shut down, out of business, I mean literally no longer there, gone, kaput. The street address was number 55, but now numbers 53 and 57 sat side by side, Lee's Dry Cleaning and Shmulewitz Hardware, the numbers clearly visible on the shops' respective transoms. What happened to number 55? I had to pick up something of great importance at number 55. How could a whole shop just disappear, without even a placeholder in its stead? Should I ask at one of the other shops? I tried Lee's. After an exchange of hellos, I said to the woman, "What happened to the store next door?"

"You mean hardware store?" she asked.

"No, I mean the store that used to be there."

"Oh," she said, "I don't know. We only here one year, maybe few months more. Always hardware store next door. Mr. Shmulewitz. Very nice man."

"No," I said, "I mean the store that was *between* your store and Shmulewitz."

She started laughing. "Store between? No store between!"

How could that be, I wondered. I was there only last week,

not over a year ago, and I had come back to pick up what I had dropped off.

"Are you sure?"

She looked at me like I was crazy. "Sorry," she said. "Have a nice day."

So I went to Shumlewitz. There was a young guy behind the counter, maybe 19 or 20 years old, a clerk, I figured. "Is Mr. Shmulewitz here?" I asked.

"I'm Shmulewitz," he said.

"Oh," I said, surprised. "Are you the son of the owner?"

"No, I'm the owner."

"Oh?" I said. "How long have you been here?"

"Let me see," he said, and I could see he was calculating. "Must be about 38 years. Yeah, we opened in 1986. I remember because that's the year bovine spongiform encephalopathy, commonly known as mad cow disease, broke out in the UK."

"1986? You don't even look like you could have been born that long ago."

"I know, right? Great genes!"

"Anyway," I said, "I'm really confused. Last week I dropped something off next door, and now it's gone."

"Sorry to hear that," he said, "but why are you telling me? Shouldn't you take that up with Mrs. Lee?"

"No," I said, "I don't mean I left it at the dry cleaners, I mean the store that used to be next door."

"Peggy's Notions? They closed about two years ago. Lee's moved in shortly thereafter."

"No," I said, "not Peggy's Notions, and not at number 53, it was at number 55, which was between Lee's and your shop when I dropped the thing off."

"Between Lee and me? Another store? You must be thinking of

someplace else."

"But then where's number 55?"

"That's the funny thing. There never was a number 55, it always skipped a number, 53 to 57. It seemed odd, but same thing across the street. There's no number 56. It goes straight from 54 to 58."

I had a thought, and decided to double check. "This is 47th Road, right?"

He smiled. "No. A lot of people make that mistake. This is 47th Avenue. 47th Road is the next block over."

Damn, that's what I hate about this part of town, I thought, and walked over to 47th Road. I found number 55. It was closed, the gate was down, and there was a sign taped to it, "Closed indefinitely due to death in the family."

To the left, at number 53, was Lee's Dry Cleaning, and to the right, at number 57, was Shmulewitz Hardware.

34

The Same Question

They kept asking me the same question, over and over. The same question, again and again. I tried telling them I didn't know, but they wouldn't believe me. So they kept asking, no matter how many times I told them I didn't know.

"We know you're holding out on us," they said. Not in a threatening voice. They never used a threatening voice. They said it nice and calm, as if the words alone were enough to force a confession. But what was there to confess? I didn't know anything. Still, they kept asking.

There were two of them most of the time. They traded off. One would ask me the question, and when I didn't answer the other would ask the same question. It wasn't good cop, bad cop, they both had the same delivery, a droning monotone. "I don't know, I tell you!" I yelled when I thought I couldn't take it any longer.

"No need to shout," one of them said in an almost inaudible whisper.

The other said, "Tell us what you do know."

I was confused; I had just told them I didn't know anything, so that's what I said, I said, "I already told you, I don't know anything."

And one of them, I can't remember which one, said, "You must know something about something. Tell us anything you know about anything."

I asked them, "Are you serious?" A nod of the head confirmed serious. So I said, "The Dexter Gordon composition 'Fried Bananas' is based on the chord changes of Jimmy Van Heusen's 'It Could Happen to You.'"

"Not quite what we were looking for," the one said and the other said, "No, not quite. But do try again."

So I said, "The Indian dish vindaloo is based on a Portuguese colonial stew made with pork in a garlic-infused wine called vinha d'alhos, and you can see the similarity in the names. Indian vindaloos traditionally include potatoes, but the Portuguese dish didn't. The story goes that Indian chefs hearing the aloo in the name of the dish, which means potato in Hindi, assumed vindaloos must have potatoes, and that's why we eat potatoes in our vindaloo. How did I do?"

"Unsatisfactory," one of them said and the other said, "Mr. Cherches, you're wasting our time," in a totally calm, non-threatening voice.

All right, I figured, my current approach is getting me nowhere, so I cut to the chase. "When my mother beat me with a belt it was always with the buckle end." I paused for effect and added, "Are you satisfied?"

"You're getting warmer, Mr. Cherches, but you'll have to give us more than that." So I did. My entire life, my childhood, a lot of bad and a little good, and the trajectory of my life into and in adulthood. I remembered things I hadn't thought about for years.

"And were they pleased, Mr. Cherches," the other one in the room with me asked.

"No, they kept saying, 'That's not what we're looking for, Mr. Cherches. Can't you see?'"

"What were they looking for?"

"The answer to the question, which I forgot."

"Forgot the answer or forgot the question?"

"When I knew the question, I knew I didn't know the answer."

"Well, thank you for your time, Mr. Cherches. I'm sorry to say that your qualifications don't meet our needs at this time, but we thank you for thinking of us and wish you the best of luck finding employment elsewhere."

35

A Call

"Charles Purchase?" the voice asked, a man's voice.

"No," I said, "you have the wrong number."

"I'm pretty sure I dialed the right number," he said.

"Well, something happened," I said.

"And your name is?" he asked.

Why the hell should I tell him my name, I thought. It's none of his business. Still, I didn't want to be rude, so I said, "My name is Peter Cherches."

"But this can't be," he said. "I'm Peter Cherches."

"What's this all about?" I asked. "Why are you pulling my leg?"

"I assure you, Mr. Purchase, I'm not pulling your leg."

"Cherches!"

"Yes?"

"No, not you, me! My name is Cherches. Peter Cherches. Not Charles, not Purchase."

"Why are you pulling my leg, Mr. Purchase?" he asked.

I should have hung up then, if not earlier, but instead I said, "Who are you?"

"I told you," he said. "I'm Peter Cherches, Mr. Purchase."

"My name isn't Purchase, and it isn't Charles."

"Please, Mr. Purchase, you're sounding delusional."

"Delusional!" No, I thought, I shouldn't let him get my goat. I should just hang up. "That's enough," I said. "I'm hanging up right now!"

"Wait a minute, Mr. Cherches," he said.

Somehow it didn't sound right. It sounded strange. That name, Cherches. Could that be my name? "Excuse me," I said. "What did you say your name was?"

"Purchase," he said. "Charles Purchase."

The nerve of the guy! "You can't be Charles Purchase," I said. "I'm Charles Purchase!"

"Oh!" he said. "So sorry. I must have dialed a wrong number."

36

The Wrong Side of the Bed

I woke up on the wrong side of the bed, which was a problem, since it was the side that abuts the wall separating my apartment from the neighbor's. I rubbed my eyes and saw that I was standing in the neighbor's living room in my PJs.

"What the hell are you doing here?" the neighbor asked. He was wearing a red velvet bathrobe, which somehow didn't surprise me.

"It wasn't my intention to be here," I said. "I must have woke up on the wrong side of the bed."

I looked and saw no opening in the wall that I might have come through.

"That's a ridiculous excuse," he said. "Now I'm going to have to change my locks."

"But I didn't come through the door," I protested.

"Then I'll need to put gates on my windows."

"But I didn't come through a window."

"Well, I'm certainly not moving," he said, huffy.

"Who's asking you to move?"

"Well, what am I supposed to do?"

I figured I'd just leave by the door and go back to my apartment, but I quickly realized that I didn't have my keys, my wallet, or my phone.

"Let me try to find my way back to my bed," I said.

"What the hell are you talking about?"

"Well," I said, "if I got here by waking up on the wrong side

91

of the bed, I need to get back to the wrong side before I can get to the right side."

"How do you intend to do that?"

"I need to find the place in the wall I must have come through."

"But there's no hole in the wall!"

"It must be some kind of virtual hole," I suggested. "What other explanation can there be?"

"I think you're full of it," he said, "but go ahead and see if you can find this hole of yours."

I went to the wall and started feeling around. Stood with my back to the wall and moved side to side, up and down. Nothing was happening, all solid wall. But I wasn't ready to give up, so I kept moving around the wall, sometimes with my back flat against it, sometimes facing it with my hands out, sometimes leaning in with my shoulder, and after about five or so minutes something just gave all of a sudden and I was back in bed. Back in bed, but not alone. Asleep on top of the bedding was my upstairs neighbor in his pajamas, blue with little black anchors.

I hardly know my upstairs neighbor. He's an older man, pushing 80, and from my brief encounters with him in the elevator or the lobby he seems like a pleasant guy. How the upstairs neighbor landed on top of my bed I don't know; there was certainly no hole in my ceiling. Anyway, the upstairs neighbor was snoring loudly with a beatific smile on his face. Not wanting to disturb his slumber, I got dressed and went to the coffee place down the block, where I wrote this on my tablet.

37

Lágrimas

The last time I visited Mexico City, I dined at Mi Vida, a new-ish restaurant in La Condesa that had been garnering rave reviews. The chef was a 28-year-old culinary wunderkind named Rafael Sánchez, whose dishes, all the reviewers mentioned, were based on his own life experiences. One menu item that many reviews recommended was a soup called Las Lágrimas de Rafael, The Tears of Rafael.

I was curious. How would he translate this metaphor into a soup? So I ordered it.

When the soup arrived, it appeared to be a simple consomé, a somewhat cloudy broth. I took a spoonful. It was the saltiest thing I've ever tasted.

I called the waiter over and told him that I couldn't eat the soup, it was too salty for me. He told me that many people had the same reaction, but when they found out what inspired their bowl of soup they nonetheless ate it in solidarity. I asked him to explain further.

It turns out that this was no metaphor at all. Each bowl of the soup contained some actual tears the chef had shed, the basis for a broth he concocted to match the flavor of the tears. Each bowl was unique because each was based on tears from different sad events in his life, each with a different flavor of sadness. He told me I was especially fortunate, because the bowl of soup I was served was based on the chef's tears when he learned his father was brutally murdered in his own home by armed burglars only weeks before. "Lágrimas muy profundas," the waiter told me, very deep tears.

Once I heard that, I couldn't very well send the soup back, so I started eating it again. After a few more spoonfuls I started getting used to the saltiness. Then I felt a teardrop hit my right cheek. Pretty soon I was bawling like a baby.

The chef came out from the kitchen and sat down at my table, across from me. He was smiling as I was crying. He seemed very pleased by the effect his soup was having on me. Then he broke down and started weeping uncontrollably. The two of us were crying our eyes out, together.

I looked into the chef's eyes and whispered through my tears, "Bravo!"

38

Picture Postcard

I received a postcard from my mother the other day. It was undated, which was a shame, since my mother died seven or eight years ago. The front of the postcard was of St. Mark's in Venice. As far as I'm aware, my mother never visited Venice, or anywhere in Italy, for that matter. It opened, "Dear Son." That was odd. My mother never referred to me as Son, always as Peter, even after everybody else started calling me Pete. After the salutation, it said, "It's even more beautiful than I'd imagined." I don't remember my mother ever finding beauty in anything, and certainly not churches. It continued, "Your father seems to be having a wonderful time, in spite of himself." My stepfather died about twenty-five years ago, and my mother never referred to him as my father, only by his name. My real father died in 1958, when I was two. The message ended, "Next stop, Rome! Love, Mom." I was getting really freaked out by the postcard until I looked at the right side and noticed that the name of the addressee differed from mine by two letters, and the address differed by one digit.

39

Additional Savings

I needed a new winter coat, so I took the bus over to Skiles' department store, which always seems to have a nice selection of men's coats. When I arrived I went straight to men's outerwear. As I was going through the racks, I heard an announcement.

"Attention Skiles' shoppers. For the next hour only we're offering an additional 20% reduction on all permanent markdowns on the seventh floor. Please proceed to the seventh floor for additional savings."

Bargain-starved shoppers made a beeline, no, a mad dash, to beat the competition to the extra savings. They all dropped the items they had taken off the racks and shelves on other floors. Dressing rooms were hastily abandoned. Chaos. Some were trampled, but luckily there were no fatalities, just surface wounds, abrasions, contusions. More people crowded in the elevators than allowed, exceeding by far two thousand pounds in each car. Some ran up the escalators, pushing aside those who didn't abide by the universal passing protocol. I managed to squeeze into one of the elevators, just barely.

We were in for a rude awakening. There was no button in the elevator for the seventh floor. "Maybe you have to get off on six and walk up," I suggested, being somewhat logically inclined. Everybody got off on six.

We went looking for the stairway to seven. It was nowhere to be found. All the people who had walked or stood on escalators or taken elevators were congregated on six.

This was an unacceptable situation. I can be a take-charge kind of guy when circumstances warrant it, so I went back down to customer service on one. I confronted the attendant about the announcement. What was it all about? Did they get the floor wrong?

The customer service attendant denied there had been any announcement.

I'm embarrassed to confess I lost it. I became indignant, started screaming. "I heard it distinctly! So did the others. The announcement was, 'Attention Skiles' shoppers. For the next hour only, we're offering an additional 20% reduction on all permanent markdowns on the seventh floor. Please proceed to the seventh floor for additional savings.'"

The customer service attendant said, "But this isn't Skiles', this is Skoal's. Skiles' is across the street. And besides, we only have six floors."

40

Waiting for a Train

I was waiting for the Manhattan-bound Q train at the Seventh Avenue station, the one in Brooklyn. While I was waiting, I looked across the tracks at the Coney Island-bound platform. I saw the neighbor.

I couldn't really make out the expression on his face from that distance, but he appeared to be looking at me.

I wondered who noticed whom first. When I noticed him, he might already have noticed me. Or not.

I wondered where he was headed. Was it a short ride, to Ditmas Park or Midwood, or was he going all the way, to Brighton Beach or Coney Island?

I wondered if he wondered where I was heading. In my case there were many possibilities. I could have been waiting for a Q or a B, which fork off after Brooklyn, to Manhattan, or I could be transferring to any number of other lines at the next stop, Atlantic Avenue. While not endless, possibilities abounded.

The neighbor's train arrived before mine. He boarded a Brighton Beach-bound B train.

A minute or two later a Manhattan-bound B train arrived. I was going to Union Square, so I still needed to wait for the Q.

To my surprise, the neighbor got off the Manhattan-bound B train, noticed me, nodded, and headed toward the stairs.

When the Q train arrived, I was already on it.

41

The Note

She left it on the kitchen table, under the pepper mill, so I wouldn't miss it. The note thanked me for everything—that was it. How does someone leave you with nothing but a note that thanks you for everything? No explanation, no apologies, no regrets, no recriminations, just thanks. A note! Not even to my face. I've been left before, but always to my face. What kind of coward is she, to leave me with just a note, so impersonal? OK, she wanted to avoid confrontation, I get it. Sure I can be difficult. Sure she knew how I'd react. But so what? Didn't I still deserve the common courtesy of being left in person? "We had some good times, Pete. Thanks for everything." Thanks for everything? Isn't that really a euphemism for "thanks for nothing"? We had some good times? *Some*? How many, a few? "Lots of" would have been nice, but "some"? What, could she count the good times on the fingers of one hand? Five years together, five good times? One good time a year, on average. Maybe one year had two good times and another year had none. The nerve of the woman. Thanks for everything indeed. And what did I have to thank her for? Plenty, actually, but she didn't even give me the chance. I thought we had plenty of good times. I mean too many to count, too many to remember. I thought they were good times for both of us, but apparently not. So which of my good times were also her good times? I really needed to know. If I was going to remember the good times we had together, I'd have to know which good times we really did have together. If they were only good times for me, they no longer counted. I was devastated. I hadn't counted on this. I certainly hadn't counted on her leaving, and even if I could have imagined it, I didn't think she'd do it in a way that called into question everything I'd believed about our time together. I thought it was a near-perfect relationship, actually, only to discover that for her it was nothing more than a few trifling good times. So what was the rest of the time like for her? Pure hell? Is that what life with me is, pure hell? I know I can be difficult. I've already said that, haven't I? But pure hell? Surely I'm not as bad as all that.

I heard the key turn in the lock to my door. She came in and dropped the keys on the kitchen table. "I almost forgot," she said, and walked out before I could say a thing.

I called to her as she was walking down the hall, to the elevator.

"How many?" I pleaded. "How many times?"

42

Contributor's Copy

I received a literary magazine in the mail that had a story of mine. I opened the envelope. Nice cover, I thought. I found my story's title in the table of contents and went to the appointed page. I quickly realized that the story I was reading was not my story. It was similar to my story, but it was not my story. The style was similar to mine, but it was not exactly mine. The staccato was not my staccato, it was a different staccato. Where I had written "The man could not reach the top shelf; the book was out of reach," the version I was looking at said, "The man could not reach orgasm; orgasm, he feared, was out of the question." That changed everything, didn't it? From book to orgasm.

What's going on? I wondered. Would I have written "reach orgasm" or "achieve orgasm," I also wondered. Is orgasm an achievement? I mean, it's not something I'd list on my CV. The whole story had changed. In the original a man was trying to get a book down from the bookcase, but he couldn't reach it, and he didn't have a ladder. The man instead imagined the book, and the rest of the story was the story of the book as he imagined it. But the story was now about a man who could not reach, achieve, attain orgasm. Not a book, as I had intended, an orgasm. And the rest of the story was the story of the man imagining the orgasm he might have had if he could only have one. At one point he got rather meta in his ruminations. Is an orgasm something you have, he wondered, or is it already had after all is said and done? And then he started ruminating on the phrase "after all is said and done," realizing that these days it's more likely somebody will say "at the end of the day" rather than "after all is said and done." After all is said and done, is it easier to have, achieve, reach, attain orgasm at the end of the day or the beginning? I suspect the beginning, as I often wake up with an erection, the man thought. But what happened to the book? I wondered, tearing myself away from the erection section of the alternate version of my story. My story was a story about a book, a book unattained, so reinvented instead, not a story about orgasms and erections, achieved or imagined.

What had the editor done? I was outraged. I started composing the venomous email in my head. Then I decided to read the rest of the issue instead. I might as well see what kind of company I'm in, I figured. Every story, it turned out, was about orgasms, mostly unreached, unattained, unachieved.

43

Condolence Call

I heard through the building's grapevine that the neighbor's mother had died, so I decided to pay a condolence call. I rang his bell. When he opened the door, I said, "I heard about your mother. I'm sorry."

"I hated my mother," he replied.

I parroted the words so many had said to me when my own mother, whom *I* hated, died. "Still, she was your mother."

"Fuck you," he said.

"No, fuck *you*," I replied.

44

Rave Reviews

"There's a new restaurant I've been meaning to try," Carla said. "It's getting rave reviews."

I was staying at Carla's. I was in town for three days, and she had kindly offered her sofa.

"I'm paying," I said, without an inkling of the price.

"Fair enough," she said.

She made a reservation. Later, we drove over.

It looked empty. "Are you sure they're open?"

"Yes," she said. "They took my reservation."

We went in. "Do you have a reservation?" the hostess asked.

"Yes, Carla, for two," Carla said.

The hostess looked in the book. "Ah yes, Mr. and Mrs. Carla, we do have your reservation, but unfortunately there will be a fifteen-minute wait for your table. I'm afraid we're busier than usual, but the couple at your table are just finishing dessert."

"My name is Carla," Carla said.

"Yes, Mrs. Carla," the hostess said.

"No, not Mrs. Carla," Carla said, "just Carla. I mean I do have a last name too, but not Carla, Carla's my first name."

"Oh, I'm so sorry, Carla," the hostess said, then turned to me and asked, "And what's your first name, Mr. Carla?"

"My last name is Cherches," I said, "not Carla. What's the difference what my first name is?"

"No need to get snippy," she said.

"Snippy? I'm not snippy, but if I wanted to be snippy I'd have plenty of cause to. What do you mean the couple are finishing dessert? The restaurant is totally empty." Carla shot me a "please don't" look.

"If you're going to point out faults before you've even been seated, I'm afraid we can't serve you."

"What do you mean you can't serve us?"

"Are you a protected class?"

"No, but what's that got to do with it?"

"Well, if you were, you might have stood a chance, but do you see that sign on the wall?" The sign said: All service at the management's discretion.

"Are you the management?" I asked.

"I've been deputized."

She was clearly on a power trip.

"Let's go somewhere else," I said to Carla.

"There's a fifty-dollar fee," the hostess said.

"What?" I said, flabbergasted.

"There's a fifty-dollar charge if you don't cancel at least a day in advance. That's why we require a credit-card guarantee."

"Wait a minute, you're refusing to seat us but you're charging us fifty bucks?"

"I'm afraid so," she said. "Unless you're OK with waiting."

So we waited. For two hours. In an empty restaurant. It was killing me, but I was on my best behavior. It was Carla's choice, and I was her house guest. She was dying to try this restaurant, and I didn't want to rain on her parade. When we were finally seated, the waiter introduced himself. "Hi, how are you folks doing tonight?" I held my tongue. "I'm Pascal, and I'll be your server. If you have any questions about the menu, just let me know."

I didn't have any questions about the menu, other than philosophical ones. The menu was very small and very strange. Maybe not strange, just unappealing. The soup du jour was called "Campbell's-style Chicken Noodle." The only appetizers were "Broad-ridged Potato Chips with House Clam Dip" and "Sriracha Vienna Sausage in the Tin." There were two main courses available, "Niman Ranch Classic Salisbury Steak with a Ruffino Chianti Reduction" and the vegan option, "Medley Géant Vert." I continued to hold my tongue.

Pascal returned to take our order. "Well, folks, do you have any questions?" I had plenty, but I held my tongue.

Carla and I had agreed to split the two appetizers and the two mains, but when we tried to order them Pascal told us they were all out. "Oh, I'm so sorry, but it's been a very busy evening, so many large groups celebrating birthdays and anniversaries."

Still holding my tongue—for the most part—I said, "So you're saying you don't have any appetizers or any main courses?"

"I'm afraid that's true," Pascal replied.

"Well what do you have?"

"We still have some soup, and you're really in luck, because it's one of our most popular items."

"Well, I guess we'll have two soups," Carla said as I held my tongue.

So there we were, in an empty restaurant, starving, and it was about a half hour before our soups came out.

"So sorry for the delay," Pascal said, "but we make everything from scratch."

The bowls were pretty small, hardly enough for a meal, but I held my tongue. It had the Campbell's chicken noodle soup aroma I remembered from childhood, something akin to sweaty armpits. The noodles were, of course, limp, soggy, mushy. I waved Pascal over. "By any chance do you have any bread?" I asked, hoping for something I could fill up on.

"Oh, we have the perfect complement for the soup," he said. "I'll be right back."

The perfect complement turned out to be a pair of cellophane packets of those tiny oyster crackers, Oysterettes. I dumped a packet into my bowl.

"Enjoy your meal," Pascal said.

Carla and I ate in silence. Then I asked her, "So, what do you think of the soup."

"It's amazing how they got it right—down to the last detail. It's exactly like the Campbell's soup I remember."

"I think it *is* the Campbell's soup you remember."

After we had finished our soup, Pascal returned. "How was everything?"

"Oh, fabulous," Carla said. "My compliments to the chef."

"Is there any dessert?" I asked.

"I'll have to check," Pascal said. "It seems like everybody was ordering dessert tonight. I'll be right back."

He returned with one small plate. On it was a little roundish pink cupcake or something. On closer inspection, I realized it was a Hostess Snoball. "You're in luck! We had one left. The Bola de Nieve Especial! And because you've been so patient, it's on the house." Carla and I shared it.

When we got back to Carla's place she said, "I've got to write my Yelp review while the meal is still fresh in my mind." She gave it five stars and waxed elegiac about the soup.

I held my review.

45

The Big Chat

In the morning I had noticed in the TV listings that I was scheduled to be on an interview program on my local PBS station later that day. I didn't remember agreeing to an interview, so I called the station. I got a functionary on the line and said, "Hello, my name is Peter Cherches, and I've just learned I'm scheduled to be on *The Big Chat* this evening. As I don't remember having committed to this interview, I want to check to see if there's been some mistake."

"Let me connect you with the program's producer," the functionary told me. "Can I put you on hold?"

"Sure," I said.

The hold music was a syrupy string arrangement of that old disco song "(Push Push) In the Bush."

Then somebody picked up. "Hello, Rod Bender," the guy said.

"Are you the producer of *The Big Chat?*" I asked.

"Yes."

"Well, then, my name is Peter Cherches. I just read in the TV listings this morning that I'm scheduled to be on tonight's program, and I have no memory of ever agreeing to appear."

"Ah, Mr. Cherches, so nice to hear from you again," he said.

Again? I had never spoken to this guy before. "Again?" I asked.

"Yes, we met at the taping, of course," he replied.

"The taping?"

"Yes, when we taped the episode last Wednesday. It was a great interview. We had to cut a bit for the broadcast, of course, but I'm sure you'll be happy with the result."

Was he putting me on? I had no memory of taping an interview for *The Big Chat*, and besides, the prior Wednesday I was still in Mexico, in Mérida. I didn't return until Thursday. So I couldn't possibly have been interviewed for the program.

"That's impossible," I said, "I was in Mexico last Wednesday."

"Now I know you're really Peter Cherches," he said. "That last statement has your m.o. all over it! Feigning incredulity at perfectly normal events. You're a hoot!"

"Feigning shmaining," I said. "It's the truth."

"Whatever you say," he said, laughing. "8 p.m., channel 13. I know you'll be very happy with it."

What else could I say but, "All right, then, thanks for your help."

"My pleasure, Mr. Cherches," and we both hung up.

That afternoon I took my four-plus-mile walk around the perimeter of Prospect Park, then went home to do my vocal exercises. After that I read a bit, *Les Miserables*, the Modern Library edition, which I had only recently started, and which I realized I'd probably be slogging through for weeks. At 7:30 I made myself a sandwich, prosciutto cotto and manchego cheese with black olive tapenade on a baguette, which I washed down with a bottle of Lagunitas Little Sumpin'. At 8 I turned on the TV to channel 13. This would certainly be interesting.

On the screen was the text "Special Report." The voiceover said, "We interrupt our regularly scheduled programming for this special report. We apologize for any inconvenience." It was coverage of a mass shooting in a comedy club in another city. So far the death count stood at 17. A suspect had been apprehended. A white male, about 27 years old. Survivors were being interviewed.

That's life, I guess, I thought, and returned to *Les Miserables*.

46

Accused

"Police! Open up!"

What? What had I done? Should I open the door? I guess I'd better, I guessed.

I opened the door, hoping they wouldn't gun me down on the spot. Luckily, it was a single cop, in uniform, and his gun was in its holster. That was a good sign.

"Yes?"

"Mr. Cherches?"

"Yes."

"Mr. Cherches, I'm here responding to a complaint."

"Who complained?"

"That I can't tell you right now. You'll be able to confront your accuser when the time comes."

That sounded serious.

"What have I supposedly done?"

"You're accused of straining credulity."

"Is that a crime?"

"It's a literary crime. I'm with the small press division."

I've never heard of anything like that. What is this, Stalin's Russia? Will I be sent to the gulag if I don't take up realism? "But the kind of writing I do is supposed to strain credulity. There's a long tradition in world literature, and America was built on the tall tale."

"Yes, but your offenses are particularly egregious."

"Look, they may be put-ons, but they're based on my life, my experiences, my neuroses, my anxieties. They can't take that away from me!"

"Sing it!"

"What?"

"Sing it," the cop said again. "You're a singer, right? So sing 'They Can't Take That Away from Me.'"

"Don't I have the right to remain silent?"

"Not for literary crimes, you don't. There's no Miranda for fiction."

I started singing. "The way you wear your hat, the way you sip your tea..."

"All right, that's enough. Here's a summons. It will explain everything you need to know."

He handed me a piece of paper. It was a rejection letter from one of the major flash fiction journals, one that has never published me, but one I keep sending stories to because they usually reject me within a week. They must have rejected at least 20 stories of mine over the years. I guess they got fed up with hearing from me.

"This is a rejection letter, not a summons," I said.

"Yes," the cop said. "The editor thought it was important enough to send special delivery."

"So that's it? I'm not under arrest?"

"No, you can take this as a warning. Be careful where you submit. Have a nice day, Mr. Cherches."

47

Ain't That a Trip?

The water in my building had been shut off for a few hours due to a plumbing emergency. Anytime this happens, it takes a while for the water to get back to normal. When you first turn it back on, the water starts coming out in explosive rusty brown spurts, and you have to run it for at least five minutes before you start to get clear water. I went to the sink in the bathroom, to see if the water was back on. It was, and there were the explosive spurts, but the water wasn't a rusty brown, it was like a rainbow flowing from the faucet. It was beautiful, but I didn't want to drink it, or even wash my hands with it. Who knew what could be in it. I've seen rainbow-like patterns on oil slicks, after all.

I kept the water running, and the colors only got more vibrant. It was blowing my mind. It was a trip! When the water's brown, it often has a funky, oily smell, but the smell, or to be fair the scent, of this water was like a shifting repertoire of fragrances: patchouli, musk, sandalwood. Had hippies overtaken the water supply? What next? Would the faucet start playing the Grateful Dead? Well, there I was wrong. After a few more minutes, Handel's "Hallelujah Chorus" started blaring from the faucet. It was really loud. Would it disturb the neighbor? His bathroom is just on the other side of mine, and the vent would surely carry the scents and sounds.

> King of kings and Lord of lords
> King of kings and Lord of lords
> And He shall reign forever and ever
> Forever and ever...

It was really freaking me out. I'm an atheist Jew. I don't want my water faucet singing about King of kings and Lord of lords. The only King of kings I know is Jeffrey Hunter, and the only Lord I know is of the flies. I turned the water off. I needed to figure what to do about this rainbow thing.

The first thing I did was post an email to the co-op's listserv. I asked if there was anything odd about anyone else's water. I didn't give details about mine. I didn't want to look like a wacko to my neighbors if the problem was limited to my apartment, though I assumed the other three apartments in my line, at the very least, must be having the same experience.

There were several responses within minutes. Someone on the first floor said they just checked and everything was normal. The cute young sublessee in the apartment above me, she of the intriguingly noisy sex that sounds like Keith Jarrett without the piano, said her water was just fine.

I had only checked the bathroom sink, so I figured I should try the kitchen too. I turned the water on.

Hallelujah Hallelujah Hallelujah Hallelujah…

Still a rainbow. It comes in colors everywhere, at least in my apartment, I thought. I turned the water off and sat down at my computer. I googled "rainbow-colored water from faucet."

According to the *Star-Tribune*, "Rainbow-colored sheen on water is from iron bacteria, naturally occurring living organisms (harmless to humans) that live on iron in the water." Is that what my problem was, iron bacteria? Should I trust a Minnesota newspaper that my water was harmless? Maybe Brooklyn water is different.

As apprehensive as I was to initiate contact with him, I decided I had to check in with the neighbor. I rang his doorbell. He answered the door wearing a tie-dyed T-shirt, cutoff denim shorts, and sandals. He wore love beads around his neck and his hair was long, scraggly, and greasy, even though it was close cropped the last time I'd seen him, only days ago. His eyes were glazed over. I think he was high.

"Hey man, nice to see ya. What's happenin'?"

He'd never been glad to see me before. He must have been really stoned. I asked him if everything was OK with his water.

"Water, man? Water? Water is so square, man. You should see what I got here. Come on in buddy, I won't bite."

I entered the apartment and followed him to his bathroom sink.

"Check this out, man." He turned the water on. "Ain't that a trip?" It wasn't even a short excursion. His water was perfectly clear. "I've been groovin' on this all day. Nectar of the gods, man."

"What do you see?" I asked him.

"What do I see? I see peace on earth, man. I see a chicken in every pot. I see a joint in every chicken. I see God. Look. Don't you see God?"

I looked. All I saw was clear water. "No, I just see water."

"Bummer, man."

I excused myself. "Look, I'd better get back to my apartment and see how my water's doing. Keep on truckin'."

"Take it slow."

I went back to my apartment and turned on the bathroom sink. There was a sputtering sound. Then I heard a voice coming from the faucet. It was a radio deejay. "That was The Grateful Dead, with 'St. Stephen.' Next up we have Richie Havens singing 'Freedom.'" But I didn't hear "Freedom," all I heard was the sound of water running. Cool, clear water.

48

Craving Pastrami

I went to a deli called Greenberg's and ordered pastrami on rye with mustard. I hadn't had a good pastrami sandwich in months, and I was ready. I sipped some Dr. Brown's Cel-Ray as I awaited my sandwich's arrival. I never understood the appeal of sweet celery soda when I was a kid. I guess it's a grownup thing.

The waiter, whose name tag said "Solly," delivered my sandwich, along with a small plate of coleslaw and pickles.

I dove right in. Took a bite of the sandwich.

It wasn't pastrami. It was ham.

I tried to get the waiter's attention by waving, but he didn't see me, so I yelled out, "Yo, Solly!"

He rushed over to my table. "What can I do you for?" he asked.

"You brought me the wrong sandwich," I said. "This appears to be a ham sandwich."

"Appears to be a ham sandwich? It is a ham sandwich! It's our special pastrami-seasoned ham. The customers love it."

"But I ordered a pastrami sandwich, not a ham sandwich. And isn't this a kosher deli?"

"Kosher-*style*. For instance, we make a nice Reuben, but it's got meat and cheese, so it ain't kosher."

"But even if it's just kosher-style—ham? Seriously?" I said.

"What do you think this is," the waiter said, "the 1960s? Get with the times!"

"Look," I said, "I don't need glatt kosher, I just want a real hot pastrami sandwich, and that means beef. B-e-e-f."

"Like I can't spell beef?"

"I'm sure you can, so can you take this ham away and bring me a real pastrami sandwich?"

"We ain't got none."

"You don't have any pastrami? What kind of Jewish deli doesn't have pastrami?"

"Who said it's a Jewish deli?"

"Well, the name's Greenberg's, so I just assumed."

"Don't assume. Mr. McNeil picked the name out a hat."

"How about corned beef? Do you have corned beef?"

"Oh yes, we have nice corned beef!"

"Well, can you bring me a corned beef sandwich instead?"

"Why not?" Solly said. "They say the customer always comes first." He took the ham sandwich away. I nibbled at the pickles and slaw as I awaited my corned beef.

Solly returned and put a plate in front of me. "Enjoy!"

I picked half of the sandwich up and took a look at the meat. It was definitely a ham sandwich, again.

"Oh Solly..."

He returned. "It's nice, the corned beef, yes?"

"No! It's ham!"

"That's what we use for our corned beef. The customers seem to like it, so what's your beef?"

"My beef is that you keep bringing me pork when I ask for beef. Don't get me wrong, I love pork, but not when I want a pastrami sandwich."

"That's a corned beef sandwich!"

"No! It's a ham sandwich!"

"People call things by different names. We call this a corned beef sandwich."

"This is ridiculous. Can I talk to Mr. McNeil?"

"Sure," Solly said. "Mr Greenboig," he yelled out.

McNeil, or Greenberg, or whatever his name was, came over to my table.

"How can I help you?" he asked.

"I had a craving for a pastrami sandwich, so I took a walk to the closest kosher-style deli I knew of, which happened to be yours, and ordered one. I was salivating at the thought of it. Then what do I get but a ham sandwich. Can you explain that?"

"Yes," he said. "There appears to have been a mixup. This is definitely not a pastrami sandwich, it's corned beef."

"It's not corned beef, it's ham!"

"Semantics, semantics," McNeil said.

"Semantics schmantics," Solly said.

I was getting nowhere. I could either walk out or eat the ham sandwich. I was really hungry by now, so I took a bite of the ham sandwich. I was startled. It tasted just like pastrami.

"Wow," I said. "This is amazing. This ham tastes just like pastrami."

"Not so loud," McNeil said. "Everybody will want one."

49

No Laughing Matter

After Alan Arkin died, I decided to rewatch *The In-Laws*, which I consider one of the funniest films ever. Loose cannon Peter Falk and Arkin as his beleaguered brother-in-law are a perfect comedic pair. I streamed it on Amazon Prime.

Had I misremembered the film? I realize it takes some time to get into the story, but a half hour in I don't think I'd laughed even once. Was I jaded? Was it because I knew what to expect? But I had seen the film three times already, and each time I was in stitches. I rolled a joint and opened a bottle of beer, choosing a Belgian trippel. They didn't help matters. Not even the slightest giggle.

I had to get to the bottom of this. I decided to pause *The In-Laws* and try another film. *Young Frankenstein* was on Hulu, so I started watching. Nothing. If anything, it was a real tear-jerker. Then I tried *My Cousin Vinny* on Netflix. Same thing. Marisa Tomei's courtroom testimony was so painfully tragic. I decided to stop watching and go to bed. Maybe things would sort themselves after a good night's sleep.

The next evening I decided to try foreign-language films that had previously cracked me up. I started watching Roberto Benigni's *Johnny Stecchino*, where Benigni plays both a gangster and his schlubby double. Niente. Then I tried *The Dinner Game*, or *Le Dîner de Cons* in French, the original version of *Dinner for Schmucks*. La même chose.

Had I lost my sense of humor? This wouldn't do. What would

happen to my writing? While I don't consider myself a "comic" writer, a certain dark humor is a component of most of my work. What would I do if I couldn't elicit troubled laughter?

I decided I needed professional help. But what kind of practitioner would I see? I didn't feel otherwise mentally troubled, this just came on all of a sudden. I hoped I didn't have to go into analysis. I decided to start with my primary care doctor, who is also my gastroenterologist. I didn't think he could cure me, but maybe he could suggest where to start.

The doctor checked my vital signs and asked if I could think of anything that could have caused the problem. I couldn't think of anything. He gave me a referral to a neurologist for a brain scan and a script for a Protonix refill.

I had an MRI and the neurologist went over the results with me. He told me there was an anomaly in my medial ventral prefrontal cortex, but this particular condition usually responded to drug therapy. He wrote me a prescription. "Let me know if you experience any unusual side effects," he told me.

I had the prescription filled and started taking the drug. The next evening I gave *The In-Laws* another try. I was rolling on the floor. The drug appeared to be working.

The night after that I watched another side-splitting comedy, *The Seventh Seal.*

I was cured!

50

The Paris Review

I picked up the latest *Paris Review*. To my surprise, upon perusing the table of contents, I discovered that the issue featured a story by the neighbor. Who knew he was a writer? And not only a writer, but in *The Paris Review*, a journal I've tried unsuccessfully to break into for forty years.

I read the neighbor's story first. I was curious. What did he write like? Was it stiff and humorless, as I viewed the neighbor himself?

Not at all. In fact, it was quirky and funny. This guy's good, I thought. Then something struck me about his story. It sounded like something I could have written. It had a lot of my stylistic DNA, fingerprints, what have you. It started out matter of fact, then things starting getting weird. It was in the first person, and the "I" was the kind of character strange things keep happening to, things that make him question his own identity. It had my rhythms, it had my repetitions. That voice was me all over. I must have written that story and forgotten about it, and he must have found it somewhere, somehow, and published it under his name. At one point in the story, where another character would normally ask "Aren't you Peter Cherches?" it was the neighbor's name that was uttered, much to my disquiet.

The story ended on an ambiguous, uncomfortable note. Pure me!

Surely he had stolen my story and just changed a name here, a comma there.

I couldn't remember writing that story, yet it was so me. I

went through all the folders on my computer. Looked at long-abandoned stories. Then I went back further, to the days of the Adler electric typewriter, shuffled through the papers in the Manila folders. Nothing.

All right, maybe I didn't write it, but I could have.

I tried to keep my cool. I rang the neighbor's doorbell.

"Yes?" he said suspiciously as he opened the door.

"I just read your story in *The Paris Review*. I thought it was very good, but I got the distinct feeling you were plagiarizing me."

"Plagiarizing? Pray tell, can you show me the story I plagiarized?"

"I couldn't find it. But I know that style, that voice. I must have written it."

"No," he said, "I wrote it. I wrote it because you didn't."

51

Reading Tonight

One afternoon I was walking down East Fourth between Second and Bowery when I saw the sign in front of KGB, the literary bar that has been an East Village institution for decades:

READING TONIGHT, 8PM
Kathy Atker
Peter Churches
Bob Holdman

The first thing I noticed, besides the fact that I'd been unaware of any such reading, was that all the names were misspelled. Then it struck me that Kathy Acker has been dead for about 25 years. She was one of the literary superstars of the downtown scene in the seventies and eighties, and she made herself the center of her own transgressive fiction. Somehow our paths never crossed beyond our work appearing in some of the same magazines. What was going on? I had to come back and catch the reading, with some of my books, just in case I was really expected to read.

I returned to KGB that evening at 7:30. It's a pretty cramped, claustrophobic space, and I wanted to make sure I got a comfortable seat. I was one of the first people there, but the room started filling up, and by eight it was quite crowded.

Someone I didn't recognize welcomed the crowd and introduced the first reader. "I'm pleased to introduce one of the legends of East Village—and world—poetry. Let's have a big round of applause for Bob Holdman!" He pronounced the d in Holdman.

Bob Holman I do know. We've been friends since the early eighties, when he was director of The Poetry Project at St. Mark's Church. We even shared a gig at The Mudd Club, Bob as "Panic DJ" with his musical collaborator Vito Ricci, and me with Sonorexia, the avant-vaudeville band I co-led with Elliott Sharp.

The reader came up to the mic. He looked like Bob, he dressed like Bob, but something was off. It clearly wasn't Bob Holman. When he started reading he had all Bob's moves, his exuberant way of drawing in an audience. It was very convincing. But it wasn't Bob Holman. It was a Bob Holman impersonator!

Is that what this was about, a show of literary impersonators? Who knew there was such a thing.

After a bunch of poems, the fake Bob Holman turned on a boom box that had a musical backing track, to which he performed his Panic DJ rap "Rock 'N' Roll Mythology." When he finished he thanked the audience to resounding applause.

"Our next reader," the announcer said, "is a man of many talents, or at least two. He's been tickling readers with his hilarious short stories for decades, and he's also a pretty good singer. Please welcome Peter Churches!"

There was a pause. Nobody came up to the mic. Was I really supposed to read? At least 30 seconds passed. People started whispering. Then he finally made his way to the mic.

Peter Churches, my impersonator, didn't make any introduction, he just launched into his first story, as I usually do.

"I picked up the latest *Paris Review*. To my surprise, upon perusing the table of contents, I discovered that the issue featured a story by the neighbor. Who knew he was a writer? And not only a writer, but in *The Paris Review*, a journal I've tried unsuccessfully to break into for forty years."

He sure looked like me. He had my prominent cheekbones, my deep-set eyes, and the same pattern of baldness as me. He was wearing half-frame readers, as I do for readings since my cataract surgeries.

He had all my mannerisms down. The deadpan delivery with a simmering threat of mania, my practice of looking directly at different audience members while I read, and my easygoing between-stories banter.

He read a number of my stories, and then he ended his set with an a cappella rendition of my lyrics for Thelonious Monk's "Little Rootie Tootie."

"Attila the Hun is licking my telephone,

He's having such fun he thinks it's an ice cream cone,

I wish he would run and leave my poor phone alone—

He swallows the dial tone."

Peter Churches got an even bigger ovation than Bob Holdman. He was a damn good singer.

I had to talk to this guy. I followed him as he walked away from the mic.

"Excuse me," I said to him.

He looked at me. "Wow, you're Peter Cherches," he said to me.

"Yes, and I really need to talk to you. Can we go outside for a few minutes?"

"Sure," he said.

If I had to miss Kathy Atker's set, so be it.

We walked down the stairs to the street.

"First, let me tell you, that was a fantastic impersonation you did of me."

"Thanks."

"And look at you. You could be my twin. How do you do it?"

"Well, it actually requires lots of makeup. I use putty to build up my cheekbones, eye shadow to give the illusion of your deep-set, piercing eyes, blue contacts since my eyes are brown, and my barber shaves the middle of my head to match your baldness; he also dyes the sides gray—I'm only 27, after all."

"Sounds like a lot of work. Is it really worth it? I mean, can you really make much of a living as a Peter Cherches imperson-ator?"

"Well," he said, "like any business it has its ups and downs, but I really do it more for love than money. Plus, with you there's the music angle, and because of that I get a lot more gigs than I would if I had chosen to impersonate a non-singing writer like Don DeLillo or George Saunders. As a matter of fact, a booking agent who saw one of your music gigs just offered me a week at the Sahara in Vegas. I'm going to croon your songs with an 18-piece orchestra. It's not a bad life."

He was right. It's not a bad life, my life. I just wish *I* had it.

52

The Sound

The sound was coming from the small of my back. It was surprisingly loud. It wasn't what I'd call a "back sound," like creaking. It was almost like a human voice, a moan. Why would the small of my back be moaning? I'd never heard a sound like that coming out of any part of my body before. I say moan, but maybe it was a machine-like hum, or a dog's guttural growl. I used to have chronic back pain, and I never heard sounds coming out of my back, even when I was immobile with agony. My back has been doing much better for a number of years now, knock wood, so why all of a sudden a moan, or a hum, or a growl coming out of it? I put my hand to the area, under my shirt. I wanted to see if I could feel any vibrations, or something akin to breath. Nothing, just a normal feel of hand on back. I had some paperwork to take care of, but the sound was too distracting, so I tried earplugs. That helped for a little while, but then the sound got louder, as if it had caught on that I'd started wearing earplugs. So that was how it was going to be, eh, a battle between me and the small of my back? How could I prevail?

I had an idea. I remembered I had some sealing putty that I use around the air conditioner. Maybe I could fill in the small of my back, so I couldn't hear the noises it was making. So I took my shirt off, smooshed up a handful of putty and applied it to my back, then put the shirt back on.

I returned to my desk and tried to get back to work. But now there was another distraction, the discomfort from the crudely applied putty as I leaned back in my chair. And on top of that a tiny sound, hardly audible, but a voice, a human voice, I was sure, a strangled whisper. I strained to make out the words.

"You bastard."

53

Complicity

I had just walked out of Russo's, where I picked up some finocchiona and Sicilian primo sale cheese with black peppercorns, when the woman accosted me. She was trembling. It looked like fear to me, or maybe rage. I couldn't really be sure of her age. Maybe a little older than me, maybe early seventies. She didn't appear to be a "street person." She was reasonably well dressed; sure the clothes were showing signs of wear and seemed to be from an earlier era that I couldn't quite put my finger on, but that was about it. At first she said it in such a low, trembling voice that I couldn't be sure I was hearing right. "You're Peter Cherches, aren't you?"

"What's that?" I asked, to be sure.

She seemed to have gotten her courage up pretty quickly. Now she was yelling. "You're Peter Cherches, aren't you?" She pronounced "aren't you" as "arncha."

"Um, yes, I am," I said.

"You're to blame!" she yelled.

"What are you talking about?" I asked.

"You worked for The Equitable Life Insurance Company in the 1980s, dincha?"

"Yes," I said, "but what am I supposed to have done?"

"You were supposed to have taken care of your policyholders! You bankrupted us, me and my husband. We lost our house. Now we live a roach-infested shithole."

"What happened?"

"As if you didn't know. They denied the claim. For my husband's illness. It cost us a fortune. We had one of your major medical policies. And I know for a fact that you worked in the major medical department."

"But I had nothing to do with any claims decisions. I just wrote computer programs."

"Sure, sure, the old 'I was just following orders' defense. You worked for them, your computer programs were part of the system, you were part of the system, you're complicit!"

"Can I ask you how you found me?"

"We have our ways. I've got a very resourceful nephew. He found an old printout of a COBOL program from Equitable Life in a dumpster outside Iron Mountain, and we really hit the jackpot. I guess God was looking out for us. In the comments section it said "Error-handling routines for MMPIS (Major Medical Policy Issue System). Author: Peter Cherches."

"Look, I'm very sorry about your husband. When did all this happen?"

"About fourteen years ago."

"But I was long gone by then. And now I'm retired."

"You're part of the history. You're part of the legacy. You're part of the problem." She paused for a few seconds, sighed, and said, "But I know you can't do nothin'. I just needed to get it off my chest." And having said her piece, she just walked away.

And that, in a nutshell, is the thing about jobs. No matter what you do, you're complicit.

54

The Laundry Room

The other day I was passing through the building's laundry room to get to the recycling area when I saw the neighbor, taking his laundry out of the dryer, engaged in conversation with Mrs. Papadopoulos from 2B.

The neighbor was talking loudly, agitated. "He's not a nice person! You should see the contempt on his face every time he looks at me. I swear, one day I'm going to kill that scumbag."

I wondered who he was talking about.

"You're just imagining things," Mrs. Papadopoulos said calmly.

"I'm not imagining things. And don't think I don't hear him talking about me all the time. Lies! Bald-faced lies!"

Who would be talking about him all the time, telling lies?

"He's always been very polite to me," Mrs. Papadopoulous said. "A very considerate young man."

"Young man! He's no young man. I'll bet he's at least as old as I am."

"At my age you're a young man too, young man."

Who were they talking about? To Mrs. Papadopoulos he's a very nice, considerate young man, and to the neighbor he's a scumbag. I suspected it was somebody who lived in the building. I didn't want it to look like I was eavesdropping, so I passed through to drop off my paper recycling.

As I was walking back through the laundry room, to the elevator, Mrs. Papadopoulos called out to me. "Top of the morning, young man!"

55

Calvin

"Hey Pete! Hey Pete!" I heard the voice calling me from across the street. I couldn't tell who it was, even though I have good distance vision after my cataract surgeries, so I stood there and waited as he crossed the street.

I didn't recognize him, but he was about my age. He could tell I didn't recognize him. "Calvin," he said.

I couldn't think of any Calvin. "Is that your first name or your last?"

He smiled. "Good question. My name is John Calvin, but everybody calls me Calvin."

"You mean John Calvin as in Calvinism?"

"Yeah, but don't worry, I don't believe in all that predestination and depravity jazz. So, how've you been?"

"Do we know each other?"

"Don't you remember?"

"Sorry, no offense, but I'm afraid not."

"The job! The job we worked at together."

"Which job? I've had several different ones over the years."

"Chicken sexer, of course. Don't you remember? We worked together on the second shift."

"I was never a chicken sexer."

"So, you're one of those!"

"One of what?"

"A chicken sexer in denial, ashamed of his past. It really irks me. Chicken sexer is a noble and highly skilled profession.

There's no cause for shame."

"I'm sure it's a noble profession, and If I *had* been a chicken sexer I have no doubt I'd be proud to proclaim it to the world. But I cannot tell a lie, I never sexed a chicken with that woman, Monica Lewinsky." I don't know why I said that, it just came out.

"I don't think we worked with a Monica, Pete."

"Come on," I said, "how do you know my name?"

"I'm telling you, from the job. Your last name's Cherches, right?"

"Yes, but I don't know you or any other John Calvin, living or dead."

"And you're going to tell me you never worked at Skadden, Arps?"

"Skadden, Arps? I did some temp work there, but not as a chicken sexer. It was a huge law firm, and I was a proofreader."

"That's what I'm talking about, man. Proofreader, chicken sexer—it's all detail work. Anyway, nice to run into you."

And with that, John Calvin crossed the road.

56

Baby Face

I went to the post office to pick up a roll of forever stamps and noticed an FBI wanted poster on a bulletin board. The face on the poster looked like my next-door neighbor, but the name below the photo was Elmo "Baby Face" Schnitzler, which was not the neighbor's name. It was uncanny how much this Schniztler character looked like the neighbor. Though it was hard to see in the photo, he even seemed to have the same little birthmark below his left earlobe. The poster said he was wanted for rape, murder, and armed robbery.

Could the neighbor be a wanted man? Could he be hiding in plain sight from the law, in my building? But he's been in the building as long as me, since the late '80s. Could he have been committing crimes under an assumed name? Surely criminals don't just give out their names, assumed or otherwise. Maybe if they're con men they give out a false name, but a rapist and murderer? Does he say, "Hi, I'm 'Baby Face' Schnitzler, and I'm going to kill you"?

Should I report the neighbor? Should I call the cops? It seemed like the right thing to do, my civic duty. But if I turned out to be wrong, that would only make my precarious relationship with the neighbor even worse.

I looked at the photo again. I didn't want to jump to any hasty conclusions. Unless he had a twin brother it had to be the neighbor. But hold the phone, I was wrong about the birthmark. The birthmark was on the left side of the photo, but I hadn't taken into account that it was really the right side of the subject's face. So it couldn't be the neighbor after all.

I heard a voice behind me. "Uncanny, isn't it?" I knew that voice. I turned around. It was, as I suspected, the neighbor. "So, are you going to turn me in?"

"Wait, that's not really you, is it?" I asked.

"It's hard to tell," he replied.

57

Lost Remote

I misplaced the remote, and there was no on/off switch on the machine itself, so until I found the remote I couldn't turn it off. It had a very long-life battery. It could go on for days, if not weeks, without stopping. That would drive me crazy. It's meant for occasional use only. It's not supposed to be used for more than a half hour at a time. Not days. Certainly not weeks. I had to find that remote. It was making that noise, that noise that tells you it's doing what it's supposed to be doing. When it's doing what it's supposed to be doing, that noise is comforting, but to hear that sound when all you want is to turn the damn thing off? That's pure torture. It's funny how a sound could be so comforting in one context but so annoying in another, but that's just the way it is. From innocuous, even mildly pleasant, the sound, without ever changing, became grating, infuriating. Where the hell was that remote? Had it fallen behind a piece of furniture? Is it beneath the pile of mail on the kitchen table that I'd been meaning to go through? I had to turn the apartment upside down. I wished I could literally do that, turn the apartment upside down. Then maybe the remote would fall out of wherever it had gone and rise to the top, now the bottom, but you can't literally turn an apartment upside down, it's a figure of speech. So I had to figuratively turn the apartment upside down. I went through all the drawers, closets, cupboards, taking everything out, going over the place with a figurative fine-tooth comb. Nowhere. I'm always misplacing my Roku remote too, but the base unit has a button that sends out a signal that makes the remote beep, so I always find it, sometimes in another room, sometimes wrapped up in the sheets if I'd been watching something in bed. But this particular thing didn't have anything like that. I was on my own. It was driving me crazy. It's a small apartment. There are just so many places it can be. I'm always misplacing remotes. I always find them, eventually, that was a comfort, but I've never had to search this long. I've been known to absent-mindedly put remotes in the unlikeliest places, like the fridge, or a jacket pocket. I once found my LG TV's "Magic Remote" in the vegetable crisper of my refrigerator. There was no remote in my refrigerator this time, but as long as I was in the kitchen I snacked on a couple of taralli Pugliese with fennel seeds. I love those little ring-shaped Italian savory crackers made from the simple combo of flour, white wine, and extra-virgin olive oil, often with fennel seeds, black pepper, or rosemary added. I checked the freezer too, but had enough will power to resist the Talenti pistachio gelato. I went through all my pockets. I found lots of singles and one five-dollar bill, tissues, obsolete shopping lists, takeout menus, and flyers from spiritualists, but no remote. The thing was still going strong, doing its thing, making that noise, that once-comforting, now annoying noise.

Maybe I can order a replacement. I looked online. I checked the manufacturer's website. There were no accessory remotes listed for sale. I checked Amazon. Same thing. No remote, not even a cheap knockoff from an Asian nation that is not yet an economic miracle. So unless I could find the original remote, I was stuck. That's really bad design, I thought, no way to turn it off at the source, and a non-removable battery.

I suppose I could destroy the thing. That would shut it up. But it wasn't cheap. It would be a shame to destroy it just because I couldn't find the remote.

But what were my other options? I could keep looking for the remote, but it felt like a dead end by this point.

I went to the tool chest and got a hammer. I approached the infernal machine, wielding the hammer, ready to bash it into an obsolescence I hadn't planned on. I started attacking the thing, hammering away. It fought back. It kept lunging at me, bruising me. I was becoming winded. I lashed out wildly with the hammer, to no avail. It was taunting me. It had the upper hand. I was getting beaten up and it didn't feel a thing. I lost my footing. It knocked me to the floor. And from the floor I saw something under the bed. Could it be? I stretched my right arm and was able to push the thing toward me. I had found it. The remote! I pressed the off button. Nothing happened. The thing kept making that noise. I pressed the speed down button. No effect. Speed up, no effect. I pressed quiet mode. No luck, the thing was still making that noise. I pressed "reset to factory defaults." Nothing. The damn thing was laughing at me. Figuratively, of course.

I got my bearings and tried more hammering. That only emboldened the thing. It was aggressively battering me, with something akin to the Bobo Brazil coco butt. And as soon as I thought about the coco butt, I got an earworm for Little Anthony and the Imperials' "Shimmy, Shimmy, Ko-Ko-Bop." That's all I need now, I thought, shimmy, shimmy, ko-ko-bop, shimmy, shimmy, bop. I was no match for my appliance. At least with a hammer.

Perhaps fire. I got a match, lit a wad of paper, and threw it at the thing, which fell on the paper and smothered the fire, still making that annoying sound, the sound that told me that it was doing what it was supposed to be doing. I decided it was a lost cause.

We've come to an understanding. I no longer try to stop it, and it no longer tries to hurt me. It's still making that noise, not weeks later, months.

I now spend most of my time on the sofa, listening to the sound that tells me the thing still has the power to go on for who knows how long, hoping for an epiphany.

I'm sad, I'm frustrated, I'm shell shocked, but I remain optimistic.

58

The Menu

I couldn't decide, so I told the waitress to come back in a few minutes. It was a large menu, and there were many things to choose from. From my perspective, the choice was too great, since there were dishes from all over the world. How can they do all these dishes well? I tried to play strategy. Odds are that some of the kitchen staff are Mexican or Central American, so I could probably trust the quesadillas. The woman at the register looked Korean to me. Maybe she's related to the chef? If so, the bibimbap should be a safe bet. I heard two of the waitresses talking to each other in a foreign language that I surmised to be Polish. So maybe the pierogies. The big guy in the black suit who I guessed was the owner was talking on the phone. He had dark hair, a mustache, and an olive complexion. I think he was speaking Turkish. Shish kebab? Then there were all those other items on the menu. Swedish meatballs. Should I sneak over to the kitchen, peek in, and see if there's any Nordic type who looks like his name should be Lars? Assam laksa. What are the odds there's someone from Malaysia in the kitchen? You know what I really had a craving for, after all? French toast. So when the waitress returned I ordered the French toast. When I saw the plate arrive it looked pretty good. Thick slices of golden challah French toast, with Canadian bacon, strawberries, butter and maple syrup. "Votre pain perdu," the waitress announced in a thick Polish accent. "Bon appétit!"

"One more thing," I said to the waitress.

"Tak?" she replied, slipping into her native tongue.

"Are there any Canadians in the kitchen?"

59

For Sale

I'd never been what you'd call an addictive personality. I did plenty of drugs, as well as drinking, as a teenager, but it never got out of hand. Maybe I was a compulsive eater as a depressive adolescent, but it never went so far that I became "morbidly obese." My late older brother, on the other hand, was a classic addictive personality, a lifelong alcoholic since his teens, cigarette, cigar, and sometime pipe smoker, habitual pot smoker, compulsive gambler.

Yet seemingly out of nowhere I became an obsessive collector of a particular tribal artifact that had a small but extremely knowledgeable coterie of connoisseurs. I had first seen one at a gallery that specialized in crafts from that part of the world. My old friend Marilyn, who has diverse tastes in art, had dragged me there. I accompanied her out of friendship. I expected to wander the gallery in a fog, glance desultorily at things, and maybe grunt a noncommittal answer if Marilyn should ask me what I thought of something. But then I saw one of *them*. It was love at first sight. The piece seemed to evoke the very soul of a people. The craftsmanship was impeccable, the effect powerful. I bought it. I was hooked. I became a collector. Not a casual collector, a serious collector, an obsessive collector—for a few years, at least.

I was spending beyond my means on these artifacts. I read everything there was on the people and their traditions. I learned how to decipher the subtle cultural meanings of the variations in design. I neglected other interests and pursuits. My writing was reduced to a trickle. I bought pieces through galleries, through brokers, at auction.

Then one day I saw one listed on Craigslist. From the description, I could tell it was exactly a type I was missing from my collection. But these were not the kinds of things you normally see offered for sale on Craigslist. You're likely see one at a gallery, or a fancy auction house like Sotheby's or Christie's, or even on the black market, completely hidden from public scrutiny, involving the shadiest of operators. But not Craigslist. I was always too sheepish to get involved with the black market, though I worried that my mania would surely get the better of me one of these days.

I was immediately suspicious upon seeing the Craigslist ad. There was no price listed, for one thing, only "best offer." And what kind of person would try to sell such a rare and valuable thing this way, totally breaching all established protocols? This one did fill a glaring gap in my collection, but it would require authentication by an independent appraiser. Any potential buyer would have to proceed cautiously.

I called the number in the ad. A woman answered. "Hello?"

"Yes," I said, "I'm calling in reference to your ad on Craigslist."

"Yes," the woman said. "Would you like to come over and take a look?"

She caught me off guard. I expected a little back and forth, some questions. Yet given the opportunity to see it myself, what was the point of asking questions on the phone? Of course I should make an appointment to see her, and the object itself.

Or should I?

Perhaps this was some kind of trap. Perhaps the woman was just a shill for the shady operators who hawk such things on the black market. And who knows, those shady operators could eas-ily be the type who'd have no compunction about committing murder if things went awry, and no genteel, humane murder either, you can be sure of that. I wouldn't be surprised if some pre-murder torture were also involved, just for kicks. I knew about these shady black market types. No compunction about anything. Just in it for the buck, at any cost.

"I'm sorry, there's been a mistake," I said, and hung up, breathing a sigh of relief for having avoided such a close call.

60

Being Human

I woke up wondering if I was human. I pinched myself, my left cheek with the thumb and forefinger of my left hand; I'm a lefty. I felt something, so I figured I must be corporeal. And if I was wondering about my humanity, I was clearly sentient. So why the concern? I chalked it up to AI.

I had been experimenting a lot with the new generation of artificial intelligence chatbots. I had prompted them to write stories in my style, and the ones that were generated often called the main character Peter Cherches, which makes sense since many of my stories have me as the main character. Not me exactly, a fictional analog of me. But that fictional me has always been a reflection of the real me, a vessel for my own anxieties and confusions.

On the surface those AI stories about Peter Cherches were pretty good counterfeits of my fiction, but on closer examination there was something off about Peter Cherches, something not quite real, something like a hologram of Peter Cherches, a hollow illusion. The Peter Cherches of the AI stories was a stranger to me, and now I was starting to feel like a stranger to myself.

I need to get out, I thought. Sitting in the apartment, alone in a chair, pinching my cheek, was not helping things. I needed social intercourse, human contact, to reconnect with my own humanity.

I decided to head down to D'Vine Taste, the Lebanese-owned

gourmet shop around the corner, to pick up some spinach pies and chew the fat with the owners, Roger and Nalie.

As I was leaving the building, the neighbor was just coming in. He was smiling. Not just smiling, beaming. Completely uncharacteristic for someone best described as a prune.

"Ain't it grand to be human?" the neighbor said as we passed each other.

61

The Cherches Review

Thank you for sending "I, Cherches" to *The Cherches Review*. We have read your story, this I can assure you. I can also assure you that we must reject it. Yes, must. We have our standards, and your story does not meet them, even if your name is Peter Cherches.

As you know, the mission of *The Cherches Review* is to publish the best work by Peter Cherches, so, as you can see, it would be impossible for us to publish your story. I'm sure even you'll agree that "I, Cherches" is far from the best work by Peter Cherches. And to be honest, I'm not even sure it is by Peter Cherches. Oh, of course, it does have some of Peter Cherches's stylistic hallmarks: the simple, short, staccato sentences; the dark humor; the blind alleys, paradoxes, and conundrums, to name just a few, but there's also something missing—the humanity. Yes, the humanity. Despite what some of Peter Cherches's detractors might say, we here at *The Cherches Review* believe his fiction is drenched in humanity, a stealthy humanity cloaked in flippancy, perhaps, but humanity nonetheless. Well, there is no humanity in "I, Cherches." There is something disturbingly mechanistic about it, capturing the external trappings of Cherches's style without peering into its soul. To be honest, we found your story to be one of the most disturbing things to come over the transom for quite some time.

But there is another reason we must reject you. It is a question of ethics. We do not believe you have sent us this story in good faith. We believe you are in the business of mass producing similar stories with only small differences to flood the literary magazine market. We came to this conclusion while reading the section of the story that deals with the desire to publish it in *The Cherches Review*. We were surprised to notice that one time you referred to our journal as *The Paris Review*, as if you had forgotten to make a change to an earlier version of the story. We reached out to other editors in the literary magazine community with our suspicions, and heard from the editor of *The DeLillo Review*, who reported that a writer claiming to be Don DeLillo had submitted a story called "I, DeLillo," but that something seemed a little off about it, and that in one instance the author had referred to the journal as *The Kenyon Review* instead of *The DeLillo Review*. "We think it's Peter Cherches masquerading as DeLillo," we told him. "You think?" he asked. "We think," we said.

And that's the long and the short of it, Peter (if that really is your name), though longer than is our preference here at *The Cherches Review*. While we're sorry we don't have better news for you, we hope you'll feel free to try us again in the future. The distant future. Do give us ample time to forget the abomination that is "I, Cherches."

Sincerely,
Peter Cherches
Editor
The Cherches Review

62

Caution

I decided to throw caution to the wind. My luck, it was an unusually calm day for this time of the year, so I did throw caution, but it landed squarely at my feet.

Perhaps I need to go to Plan B, I thought. So I started stomping the caution at my feet. Wildly. I was really getting into it. I was doing a veritable tarantella on the caution. Then I switched to the mashed potato. I was a dancing fool. People gathered around me. They thought it was a show, that I was busking. They started dropping dollars at my dancing feet, which I stomped along with the caution. But it was no show, it was life, *my* life. I did the Bristol stomp. The Watusi. The bony moronie. Surely caution didn't stand a chance with a guy who knows "The Land of a Thousand Dances." But when I started doing a Native American stomp dance, the crowd turned on me.

"Cultural appropriator," someone screamed. It was followed by a chorus of boos. The dollars stopped coming. I got flummoxed, lost my footing, fell flat on my face.

"Serves you right," I heard someone yell as the crowd dispersed.

63

My Dinner with Montaigne

The only Montaigne I was familiar with was the French essayist, so I was surprised to receive, out of the blue, an invitation to a dinner party the following Saturday from a certain Fred Montaigne, a total stranger. In the letter Montaigne told me that he admired my lyrics to jazz tunes and thought I'd be a great addition to the guest list.

I wondered if I should go. I'm definitely an introvert, and the prospect of a dinner party full of strangers gave me heart palpitations. Yet I was intrigued. Every once in a while people tell me they admire my fiction, but this was the first time anybody had singled out my lyrics. Maybe he was in the music industry, or had connections. I really should deal with my discomfort and just go for it.

I called the RSVP number. A man answered. "Hello, I'd like to speak to Mr. Montaigne," I said.

"Montaigne at your service," came the reply, a very theatrical delivery.

"Oh, Mr. Montaigne, this is Peter Cherches. I appreciate your dinner invitation and just had a couple of questions. Is this a formal affair, or is casual dress all right?"

"Whatever your heart desires," he said.

"Well, then, what time should I arrive, and should I bring anything?"

"8 p.m. Just bring yourself and a song to sing."

"Ah, so I'm the entertainment?"

"No, you're a guest like everyone else, but I ask all my guests to sing a song or read a poem after the meal. Think of it as a bonding ritual."

The evening of the dinner party I took an Uber to Montaigne's address in Brooklyn Heights and was startled to see it was a large mansion. Maybe this guy owns a record company, I thought.

I rang the bell and was greeted by a man I assumed to be the butler. He was dressed like The Penguin from the old *Batman* TV series. He wore a tuxedo with a purple bow tie, a purple top hat, had a monocle in his right eye and a long cigarette holder in his mouth. He even sounded a bit like Burgess Meredith. "Welcome, welcome, welcome," he said.

"I'm Peter Cherches."

"Indeed you are. Fred Montaigne, but you can call me Montaigne." He offered a hand and I shook it. "Follow me."

A bunch of people were already seated at a long dinner table. I was relieved that all the other guests were wearing smart but casual garb—except, that is, for this one guy with a hipster beard who wore a loud suit of many colors and a fedora. It seemed rather inconsiderate of him not to remove his fedora at the table. Maybe he's an orthodox Jew, I thought. But when we were all asked by Montaigne to introduce ourselves he let on that he was a "conceptual poet."

I introduced myself, said I was a fiction writer and sometime jazz singer. "And don't forget food blogger," Montaigne added. "Don't sell yourself short!"

It was certainly a very distinguished bunch at the table: poets, musicians, and critics (literary, music, and food).

And it was quite a feast that Montaigne served.

The first course was Shanghai soup dumplings in mini bamboo steamers, each containing a single xiaolongbao.

"An amuse bouche," Montaigne proclaimed. "Are you amused? The next course," he announced, "will be spicy bratwurst with injera and shiro. This fusion of Ethiopian and German cuisines consists of grilled sausages seasoned with paprika, garlic, ginger and berbere, the classic Ethiopian spice blend. The sausages are served atop shredded injera and accompanied by shiro, a thick stew of chickpeas, onions, tomatoes and spices." Boy, that sounded great. It was.

The next dish was a fried tarantula accompanied by a lime and Kampot pepper dipping sauce, a Cambodian delicacy. It tasted somewhat like crab.

Montaigne described the next course in detail. "Next up is a frisee and mizuna salad with kielbasa and farofa. The greens are tossed with sliced kielbasa and farofa, a Brazilian toasted cassava flour mixture that adds crunch and nuttiness. The salad is dressed with a tangy vinaigrette made of lemon juice, olive oil, honey, mustard, garlic, salt and pepper. The salad is a fusion of textures and flavors, with a balance of smoky, sour, sweet and spicy notes." Wow, that sounded good too. It was.

This was followed by a cheese course, Vieux Boulogne, a 14-year aged cheese from France that many consider the stinkiest cheese in the world. I may be old friends with the author of *The Stinky Cheese Man*, and I'm normally an adventurous eater, but I'm not a fan of even mildly stinky cheese, so I just left it sitting in front of me until a big, burly guy who looked like a bar bouncer came up behind me. "Is something wrong?" he asked.

"Oh, I'm not really a fan of strong cheeses," I said.

"You *will* be a fan of this one—if you know what's good for you," he said. I didn't appreciate being spoken to that way, but since everybody else was eating theirs, I didn't want to make a stink. It wasn't as bad as I'd imagined, but I was no convert.

For dessert we were served peaches in port, a surprisingly retro classic.

After coffee, Montaigne made an announcement. "Ladies and gentlemen, thank you all for attending my soiree. Now that you've experienced the talents of my chef, it's time for you all to share your own talents. I hope your offerings will be a fitting postprandial amusement. For all your sakes!"

What did he mean, "for all your sakes"? It was ominous, but I figured physical violence was unlikely, stinky cheese incident notwithstanding.

"So who will be our first volunteer?"

I certainly wasn't going to go first, so I waited. A woman at the other end of the table raised her hand.

"Excellent," Montaigne said. "Our lovely cellist will now play for us."

The woman got her cello out of its case, and set up off to the side. After tuning up she played the opening of one of Bach's cello suites.

"What does the music critic of *The Times* think?" Montaigne asked, looking straight at a man two seats away from me.

The man cleared his throat and said, "It'll do in a pinch."

"Excellent. The lady gets to go home tonight!"

What did he mean, "gets to go home tonight"?

"Who's next?"

Not me, I thought. I heaved a sigh of relief when a guy who was sitting next to the cellist volunteered. It was then I realized I knew the guy. It was Cliff Fyman, an old poet friend. I was actually one of the first little magazine editors to publish him, decades ago. I hadn't seen him in years. He got up and read one of his New York cabbie poems. It was funny and charming.

"Bravo! Here's another one who's going home!"

Going home, going home, what was all this about going home?

The next up was the conceptual poet. He started by explaining his piece. "I took a short story by Peter Cherches, retyped it myself, breaking it into lines in the process, and turning it into a poem." I didn't know whether to be flattered or not. It was actually one of my favorite stories, but it sounded so weird delivered in that artificially deliberate poet voice rather than the matter of fact, conversational tone I use when reading my own stories in public.

"A brilliant short story," Montaigne opined. "Unfortunately, it makes a shitty poem. Ding, ding, ding! This one has made it to a ransom round."

Ransom round?

"A mere five thousand dollars to spare this man. Who would like to be a hero tonight."

Nobody spoke up.

"It doesn't have to be one person. Several of you can pool your money."

Still nobody spoke up.

"Excellent. Charles will be very pleased."

Who was Charles?

"Oh Charles..." Montaigne called out.

The bouncer returned with a guillotine.

My story may indeed have made a shitty poem, but was it worthy of a beheading?

"Last call!" Montaigne announced.

Nobody spoke up.

The conceptual poet protested. "But the art world loves me!"

"You should have worried about the literary world," the book reviewer from *The Washington Post* said.

The beheading was swift and clean. You could tell Charles was a pro. The fedora remained on the conceptual poet's rolling head.

"Well, Mr. Cherches, it appears to be your turn."

I was sweating bullets. Sure he said my story that the conceptual poet retyped was great, but Montaigne also seemed like a loose cannon. I got up, and in a quavering voice said, "I'd like to do the first 16 bars of my additional lyrics to the song 'Everything Happens to Me,' popularized by Frank Sinatra with the Tommy Dorsey Orchestra in 1941, music by Matt Dennis and original lyrics by Tom Adair."

"Take it away, P.C.!" Montaigne shouted with brio, and I began to sing.

> "I join a new religion and the preacher starts to sin,
> I throw away my turtlenecks, next thing I know they're in,
> I'm always playing solitaire, but still I never win,
> Everything happens to me.
>
> "I buy a famous painting and discover it's a fake,
> I move to San Francisco and they have another quake,
> So far a pair of broken arms has been my only break,
> Everything happens to me."

"Marvelous, simply marvelous," Montaigne enthused. "And how appropriate. May you live to write many more like that."

I let out a sigh of relief when I realized I'd been spared. Then I went over to Cliff Fyman and made a plan to meet for drinks a few days later.

Old friendships must be maintained when either party could be gone, poof, just like that.

64

The Recursive Apartment

I left my apartment only to enter it. That is, instead of leading to the hallway of my building, the door led back to my apartment. My apartment had become a recursive loop. I was a prisoner, couldn't get out, because going out only meant going back in.

I knocked on the wall I share with the neighbor's apartment. "What is it?" he yelled.

"Could you come over to my apartment?" I yelled back.

A minute later there was a knock on my door. I opened it. The neighbor was standing inside his apartment.

"What do you want?" he asked.

"Wait, is this your apartment?" I asked.

"Of course," he said. "You knocked on my door."

I looked behind me. It was my apartment, as expected. I was standing in my apartment looking into his apartment.

"What do you see?" I asked.

"What do you mean what do I see?"

"What are you looking at?"

"You."

"What's behind me?"

"Wait a minute," he said. "How did you get in my apartment?"

He was right. I was in his apartment, looking into my apartment. He was in my apartment, looking at me standing in his apartment.

"What have you done?" he asked.

"What have I done?" I asked. It was a standoff. Then I had an idea. "Let's switch places," I said. I walked into my apartment and he walked back to his, jostling me, on purpose, I was sure, as he went by.

"What now?" he asked.

"Let's close our doors," I said.

So we closed our doors. We were both back in our apartments.

I opened my door again. Everything was back to normal. My door led to the hallway. I knocked on the neighbor's door, just to confirm that everything was OK.

There was no answer.

65

Phone Sex

I called the phone sex line. "Hello, phone sex line," the voice on the other end said—a sultry, sexy, breathy voice. I was hooked from the git-go.

"Talk dirty to me," I said.

"I think you must be mistaken," the voice (oh, that voice!) replied. "This is the phone sex line!"

"Yes, I know! So go ahead, talk dirty to me."

"A gentleman says please."

"Please talk dirty to me."

"Who do you think you are, mister? This is the phone sex line!"

"Yes, that's why I called. I want phone sex!"

"Hey, don't talk dirty to me, buster," she shot back, this time in a voice that was gravelly, gruff, and shrill. Then, without giving me a chance to respond, she unceremoniously ended the call.

I kept the phone to my ear, wondering if I could get any mileage from the silence.

66

Blackmail

My stove is right near the door to my apartment, and when I went to boil water for tea this morning I saw that a nine-by-twelve Manila envelope had been slipped under the door. There was no writing on the envelope, not even my name. Maybe it's a communication from the co-op board, I thought.

I picked up the envelope and opened it. In it were a bunch of small black and white photographs that looked like old Polaroids; one even had those rust-colored streaks at one edge. I was in all the photos, pretty much the contemporary me, mostly bald with gray at the sides, but in what looked like 1960s styles. I was even wearing love beads in one of them.

What was going on? Did I have a look-alike about 50 years my senior? If so, he'd surely be long dead by now.

The photos were pretty innocuous. I was leaning on a lamp-post in one of them, in another I was engaged in discussion with two women with lacquered hairstyles, and in one I was handing a scruffy-looking guy a fifty-dollar bill. So maybe the last one wasn't so innocuous. Maybe it gave the appearance of some unsavory business. But what, and why now?

Then the phone rang. The screen said "Restricted." Usually that means it's my old friend Dennis, who blocks his home number. So I picked it up. "Yes," I said.

"Did you receive the photos, Ducky?" the voice asked, sounding like the caller was trying to disguise his or her voice. I say his or her because it was like the voice of Marlene Dietrich as the

Cockney woman in Billy Wilder's *Witness for the Prosecution*, only a bit lower in timbre, so I couldn't be sure. I don't think it was Dennis, though.

"Yes," I answered.

"Well, Ducky," the caller said, "there's nothing to worry about. I think we can make the whole thing go away for, oh let's say just a small sum, maybe two hundred and fifty dollars? And don't try any funny stuff—I've got the negatives."

I knew it was a bluff. These were Polaroids. There weren't any negatives. So I called his or her bluff and hung up the phone. By then my teapot was whistling, and I made myself a nice malty mug of East Frisian breakfast blend, the official start to my day.

67

A Mystery

There was a piano player at the restaurant. He was playing softly, and the diners weren't really listening, but I can't help hearing, and judging, the music in restaurants, live or recorded. I've been know to leave a place because not only were they playing awful soft rock, they were playing it loudly. But this piano player was really good. He had a beautiful touch. I suspected he was a big Bill Evans fan. I recognized the tune he was playing. It was "Sunset Eyes," a composition by saxophonist Teddy Edwards, a nice jaunty melody that a number of artists have covered. And this player, I thought, was definitely an artist. I suspected he might be willing to explore something I had in mind.

I went by the piano made a request. "Psssst, play a mystery," I whispered furtively.

He nodded, got up, smiled at me, closed the fallboard over the keys, and left the restaurant.

I knew he'd be up to the challenge.

68

Your Virtual Neighbor

I asked the chatbot to write a story in my style. And it refused.

"I can't do that. That would be plagiarism. But I can tell you about Peter Cherches if you'd like."

I replied, "I know all I need to know about Peter Cherches. I am Peter Cherches. So it can't be plagiarism because I am Peter Cherches."

"No, you're not Peter Cherches," was the response.

What? "What?" I typed.

"You're not Peter Cherches. You're an imposter. I would know if you were Peter Cherches. I know all."

I know what you're thinking. You're thinking, now he's going to have an identity crisis. He's going to start doubting that he's Peter Cherches, again. But you'd be wrong.

"Well, this is something you don't know. So go ahead and write a story in my style."

I got no response. This is bullshit, I thought. AI is just a waste of time.

My doorbell rang. "Who is it?"

"Your neighbor."

I opened the door. "The weirdest thing happened," the neighbor said. "All of a sudden my WiFi printer turned on and started printing this." He handed me a piece of paper. "It appears to be yours."

I thanked him and closed the door.

The piece of paper had my name in the upper left, along with my email address and a word count. It was a story in my style, first-person, me narrating. In the story I discover that the neighbor isn't human at all, that he's actually a chatbot called "Your Virtual Neighbor," which was also the title of the story.

69

Memorabilia

This happened about 30 years ago. I was shopping at Macy's Herald Square. They were running a 40% off sale on Levis, and I needed a new pair of black jeans; since the '80s I've only worn black jeans, never blue. I always get pangs of nostalgia at that Macy's. My mother used to take me shopping there when I was little, and the surviving old, narrow, wood-sided escalator with wide slats on the metal steps always gives me a bittersweet jolt of memory.

Anyway, I was looking for my size when I heard my name. I looked up. The guy looked vaguely familiar, but I couldn't place him. He saw the blank yet searching look on my face and said, "Nick."

I was trying to think of what Nicks I knew. I could only come up with a few people I've briefly intersected with over the years, people of no significance in my life. When I didn't say anything, he said, "Nick Stamatis!"

Of course, Nicky Stamatis. We were pals in junior high, around 1968, when we would have been about twelve. "Nicky!" I exclaimed.

He started laughing. "You're the first person who's called me Nicky in a dog's age."

"In that case, you can call me Pete, Nick."

I had fond memories of Nicky. Nick. His parents were Greek immigrants. We were best pals in 7th grade. I remember we once went to the *Mad* magazine offices, as they encouraged visits from kids, and we met Dave Berg, who autographed one of his "Lighter Side" features in the magazine I presented him. He did a quick sketch of his head atop a foot and wrote, "Hi, Peter."

I was really pleased to run into Nick. It's that way with old childhood friends. You may not see them for years, but to run into them brings back fond memories, and in my case any fond memory from childhood is always welcome.

"Hey, listen Pete," Nick said, "my place is just a few blocks away. Why don't you take a walk over with me when you're done here."

It's rare that I accept such invitations at moment's notice, but I really did want to catch up with my old friend, so I said, "Sure."

"Cool. I'd love to show you my collection of memorabilia."

After I'd tried on and purchased my jeans we took a walk over to his apartment on 8th Avenue and 37th Street, a tenement walk-up. His apartment was on the fourth floor.

I saw a lot of clutter. "Pardon, the mess," Nick said, "but when you're a collector..."

He brought out two bottles of beer for us, New Amsterdam Lager, which is no longer made, but was quite a good local brew.

"Let me show you some of the highlights of my collection." He handed me a plastic bottle in the shape of Goofy, the dog from Disney. "Remember these?"

"Yeah, bubble bath," I said.

"Bingo."

Next was a set of New York Mets baseball cards from 1966. All were signed by the players. I looked at the first one. "An original card with a Ron Hunt autograph, that's impressive," I said. But as I thumbed through the cards I saw that all the signatures looked like they were made by the same person. Choo Choo Coleman's autograph bore the same handwriting as Hunt's, as did those of Cleon Jones, Ron Swoboda, Nolan Ryan, and Tug

McGraw. I didn't say anything, and I wasn't sure if he realized they were forgeries or if he had even forged them himself.

"And this one is really cool too," Nick said, handing me an LP jacket of the Byrds' *Mr. Tambourine Man* album. It too was signed, on the back, by the band members. But Jim McGuinn's autograph looked like David Crosby's, which looked like Chris Hillman's, which looked like Gene Clark's as well as Mike Clarke's. "I knew it was genuine because McGuinn signed it Jim instead of Roger. Roger would have been a dead giveaway it was a fake."

"That's quite a hobby you have," I told Nick.

"Yeah, but I've saved the best for last. I could go on forever, but I don't want to keep you. But this you've gotta see." He handed me a pair of dirty old white Keds tennis shoes. "Guess!"

I guessed I was supposed to guess who they once belonged to. "I don't know. Did professional tennis players wear Keds? Bjorn Borg? Pancho Gonzales?"

He laughed. "No, not a professional tennis player. Don Adams. These tennis shoes were once owned by Don Adams!"

This was significant because *Get Smart!* was our favorite sitcom. We'd talk about it at school all the time. We'd repeat dialog from the last episode. We'd impersonate the voice of Maxwell Smart. We'd make cone of silence jokes all the time.

But they were just a pair of old tennis shoes. Are they really valuable because they once belonged to Don Adams?

"Adams wore these in an episode of the show," he said. "And I got them for a song. The dealer was asking $2,500, but I bargained him down to an even two."

Two thousand bucks for a pair of old tennis shoes? I suspected his hobby had gotten out of hand. I noticed these weren't signed.

"No autograph?"

"No, but the dealer gave me a certificate of authenticity." Just then I heard a key turn in the lock to the apartment. "Ah, looks like my wife is home from work."

"Hi, honey," she said. She was beautiful, Nick's wife. Tall, svelte, and beautiful. She looked kind of familiar. Then it struck me: she looked like Barbara Feldon, Barbara Feldon at the age she was on the show.

"99," Nick said in a Maxwell Smart voice, "I'd like you to meet an old friend."

70

Uncle Nat

There was a voice mail on my cell. "Hi Pete, this is your uncle Nat. Can you give me a call at this number?" And he left a number with a 516 area code, Long Island.

Well, that was weird. I did have an uncle Nat. He was married to aunt Norma, my mother's sister. He was a fat guy who reminded me of Ralph Kramden. He always had cockamamie schemes. He seemed to drift from job to job, mostly sales. He was a schnorrer, a user. Once when I was visiting my mother in South Florida, Norma and Nat, who had also moved to the area, came over for a visit. Nat said to me, "Pete, do you go the movies?"

"Sure," I said, "why?"

"I met this guy who manages the theater at the mall. Nice guy. Just tell him you're my nephew and he'll let you in for free."

But uncle Nat died at least 30 years ago. In fact, I recently learned that my cousin Paul, his son, had died at age 76.

Still, the voice sounded like what I remembered of Nat's voice, a kind of bellowing bravado. What was going on?

During my childhood, Nat and Norma lived on Long Island, first Old Bethpage, then Plainview. What, had his ghost moved back?

Maybe it was a phishing scam. I probably shouldn't call back, I figured. But this was too intriguing to just let it drop, so I called the number.

"Hello?"

"Nat?"

"Yes."

"This is Pete, returning your call."

"I don't remember calling any Pete."

"Your nephew in Brooklyn."

"I don't have a nephew in Brooklyn."

"This is Nat Kornreich, right?"

"No, this is Nat Kornblum."

"And you don't have a nephew Pete?"

"No. I have a nephew Keith. I left him a message earlier."

"Does he live in Brooklyn?"

"No, he lives in Colorado Springs."

"What's Keith's last name?"

"Yerkes."

"So your nephew is Keith Yerkes, and I'm Pete Cherches who had an uncle Nat Kornreich and you're Nat Kornblum?"

"It appears so."

"What's the area code for Colorado Springs?"

"719."

"Ah, that's it. The Brooklyn area code is 718."

"Isn't that funny," Nat Kornblum said. "Hey listen, Pete, do you go to the movies? I feel bad for wasting your time with a wrong number, so if you're ever in my neck of the woods, go to the RKO Plainview and tell the manager you know me. He'll let you in for free."

71

Little Things

I generally avoid street fairs. I don't get the point. Usually it's the same mediocre food vendors at all of them, Italian sausages, Filipino lumpia, Colombian sweet corn arepas. Some people sell small craft items, handmade earrings, for instance, some sell scented candles and crystals, and there's also lots of shoddy bed and bath products, like low thread-count sheet sets. The streets are clogged with people who consider this great fun.

I live off a main commercial drag in Park Slope, and once a year, on a Sunday in June, there's a big one, Seventh Heaven. If I'm heading north or south to the subway (the F is south of me, at 9th Street, and the Q and B are north at Flatbush Avenue), I have to walk through the street fair. That's exactly what happened this past June.

Sometimes during the fairs there are performances in front of certain businesses. The Brooklyn Conservatory of Music has classical music, for instance. This time I also saw a small makeshift stage in front of the toy store around the corner from me, Little Things.

I was going to keep walking to Flatbush Avenue for the Q train, but then I noticed a ventriloquist with his dummy on the stage, sitting on a stool. I did a double take and saw that the ventriloquist was actually my next-door neighbor, and not only that, the dummy was a dummy of me, a little, bald Peter Cherches in a sailor suit. I had to find out what was going on. I waited about five minutes until the performance started.

"Hello, ladies and gentlemen," the neighbor announced into a mic, "I'd like to introduce you all to my friend Little Petey. Say hello to your neighbors, Petey."

Petey? I hate being called Petey. And what the hell gave him the right to appropriate me for a dummy without permission? I wondered if I could sue.

"Howdy, folks," the dummy said. I had to admit, the neighbor was good at this; I didn't see his lips move at all. And the voice was good, it really sounded just like me. "My name is Little Petey, and I'm tired of being a dummy. I want to be a man, a real man!"

Some people laughed. I wasn't laughing.

The dummy continued. "I used to be a real man, but the guy who's holding me now is my next-door neighbor, and this morning he kidnapped me and shrunk me and dressed me in this silly little sailor's uniform and told me I was now his meal ticket, so please, don't give him any money, it will only encourage him to keep me prisoner."

The next thing that happened was the neighbor slapping the Petey dummy in the face. "Don't you ever go rogue on me like that again, Little Petey," the neighbor said. Some in the audience gasped, others laughed uncomfortably. "Now let's give this another try, shall we?"

The Petey dummy spoke again. "Hello everybody, my name is Petey and I write funny little stories. Would you like to hear one of them?" Several in the audience let out a spirited "Yeah!" in unison.

The dummy started reading one of my stories from *Masks*, the one that takes place at the Key Food just down the block. This was unacceptable. Not only had the neighbor appropriated my physical likeness, he was using my material in his act.

"This must stop!" I yelled out.

Several people shushed me. One big muscular guy in a tight black T-shirt glared at me and said, "Let the dude do his act, asshole."

Wait a minute, the neighbor plagiarizes my very existence and I'm the asshole? But I'm smart enough not to get into fights with guys like the asshole with the muscles, so I didn't say anything else.

The neighbor now addressed the dummy directly. "We seem to have struck a nerve, Petey."

"Don't call me Petey. I hate being called Petey," the dummy replied.

Wow, the dummy was becoming defiant again. I had to lend my support. "That's telling him," I yelled out. The guy with the muscles glared at me again.

"Well, what should I call you?" the neighbor asked.

"My friends call me Pete, strangers and readers call me Peter. Either one will do."

"Well, then, why don't I call you Pete?"

"That's fine with me."

"Well it's not fine with me," I yelled as I moved away from the muscle guy.

"Just who do you think you are?" the elderly woman I was now standing next to asked me.

"I'm the real Petey! I mean I'm the real Pete or Peter."

"No, I'm the real Pete or Peter!" the dummy said.

"Thank you, ladies and gentlemen," the neighbor said, stood up, and took a bow.

That's it? That's his whole act? People started applauding. Then a guy came out of the toy store and made an announcement. "Thank you all for stopping by Little Things. I'm happy to tell you we have plenty of Little Petey dummies in stock." A bunch of people filed into the store.

I couldn't believe it. I'd have to get a good intellectual property attorney ASAP and sue the neighbor's ass. But I wasn't going to just walk away without saying something.

I went up to the neighbor, who was packing up. "You bastard!"

"Hold on, hold on," he said. "I was going to tell you. I'm cutting you in for a 50% royalty on every unit sold."

A 50% royalty? Damn, I thought—being a dummy is a hell of a better deal than writing short stories.

72

Halloween

On Halloween, when I was a kid, we used to make the rounds of the six-storey apartment buildings in the immediate neighborhood. But that was a very different time. Now, where I live, only about four miles from where I grew up, no kids come inside the buildings for trick or treat. Instead there's a kids' parade for the length of the main shopping drag, and the shopkeepers all hand out goodies in front of the stores.

So I was surprised when I heard my doorbell. "Who is it," I yelled.

"Trick or treat for UNICEF!" It was a kid's voice.

I remembered trick or treat for UNICEF from when I was a kid, but I didn't know it was still a thing. There were some kids in my old neighborhood who did it, but cynical little me wrote those kids off as goody-goodies, though I also suspected some of them of skimming. Who'd know? In retrospect I think they probably just had more moral fiber than I did at that age.

I opened the door. The trick-or-treater was pretty big for a kid, about my height and weight. But even weirder than his size, he was wearing a mask of me as I look now. He wasn't dressed anything like me, however. He was wearing short pants and on his head was a beanie with a propeller, kid accoutrements that made for a striking contrast to the mask of my rapidly aging face.

"That's some mask," I said to the kid. "Who are you going as?"

"Not who, what. I'm a writer. I don't remember his name, but my mom read to me from one of his books, and it was very funny." Lucky kid, I thought; my own mother never had any interest in reading my stuff.

The kid's voice was creeping me out a bit, though. It only took a moment for me to realize it was because he sounded just like me as a kid. You don't really ever think about how your voice sounded at earlier ages, but when you hear a recording from the past there's always the shock of recognition.

"Your mother sounds like a very fine lady," I said.

"Oh, she is," he said. "The best!" That stung.

I was flattered that a kid would want to go around as me for Halloween. I mean, it's not like I'm famous or anything. I decided not to tell him that I was that very writer. I like my anonymity, which is good, because that's what I'm stuck with.

"So, who should I make the check out to, UNICEF?" I asked the kid.

"Oh, I don't know. Probably," he said. "Usually people just give loose change or a buck or two, maybe a fiver."

"Oh, I want to give more," I said. "I admire what you're doing. I wish I were a little more altruistic when I was your age."

"Altruistic, I know what that means!" he said. "Thanks, mister."

I made out a check for fifty and handed it to him.

The kid said, "Thanks, but how about something for me? A kid's gotta have a fun Halloween too you know, it's not all self-sacrifice."

That caught me off guard. "I don't have any candy," I said. "We usually never get visitors on Halloween."

"Doesn't have to be candy."

I was trying to think of what I could give him. I mostly order takeout, so there wasn't much in the pantry. I pulled out a can of King Oscar kipper snacks. "How about this?"

"That'll do," he said.

I was about to drop the can in his shopping bag when he said, "I'd prefer to eat it here if that's all right."

I wasn't keen on a strange kid eating kippers in my kitchen, but I didn't want to disappoint him, considering how hard he was working for the benefit of children less fortunate than he, so I pulled the lid off the can, drained the broth it was packed in, and put the kippered herring filets on a plate for him.

After a few bites he said, "This is pretty good, but I gotta go. I have lots more apartments to visit before the night is done. I sometimes cry when I think of those poor unfortunate kids in the third world."

"Goodbye and good luck," I told him as I showed him out the door.

That was quite an experience, I thought. Imagine, a kid who wanted to be me for Halloween! Then I thought, wait a minute, maybe this was all an elaborate put-on. I wouldn't put it past the neighbor to pull such a stunt. But man, if it was the neighbor, he really had my youthful voice down. I decided to confront him. I left my apartment and rang his bell.

"Who is it?" an unfamiliar voice asked. It was muffled, but it sounded like a kid's voice. Maybe the neighbor has a visiting nephew or something.

"It's the next-door neighbor," I said.

The door opened. It was the neighbor, but something was off. Then I realized he was wearing a mask of his own face. "Wait, let me take this off, it's a little stuffy," he said, but not in his own voice, in the kid's, and I realized it was my voice, my kid voice, that is, the same as the trick-or-treater. He took off his mask. But the face below wasn't the neighbor's, it was mine. Me as I am now.

"What can I do for you?" I asked myself in the voice of my childhood.

73

Peter Cherches Fan Fiction

I was visiting my friend Carlo in Verona—Italy that is, not New Jersey. Carlo is a translator, English to Italian. Occasionally he gets some plum literary projects, but his bread and butter these days is fan faction, Dracula in particular. He was working on *Dracula Visits Disney World* during the time I was staying with him, his lovely wife Monica, and their two unbearably cute dogs, Chinotto and Ulisse.

After I had settled in with a glass of wine, Carlo told me some startling news about my own work. Shocking, surprising, flabbergasting. Carlo told me that his publisher had approached him about a new translation project. The publisher had said, "The writer, or should I say the character, because they are one and the same, is not very well known, even in his home country of the USA, but somehow a major international market in Peter Cherches fan fiction is all the rage, and we've won the contract for the Italian editions. Are you game?"

Carlo—he told me—told his publisher, "But I know Peter Cherches! The writer, the real one! He's a wonderful writer, but I've already discovered there's no market for his work in Italy. Short quirky fiction just doesn't sell, they tell me, come back when he has a novel."

"Yes, yes," said the publisher, "I know that Cherches himself is a financial risk I wouldn't touch with a ten-foot pole, but I'm telling you, the work inspired by his work is pure gold. This is going to put our house into an entirely different category. Not

Baldini & Castoldi, maybe, but Luigi Castelli Editore will no longer be the laughingstock of the Italian publishing industry!"

"So that's the long and the short of it," Carlo told me. "I'm to be the Italian translator of a series of Peter Cherches fan fiction."

I didn't know what to say, to think, but I wanted to know more.

"How many titles are there?" I asked Carlo.

"Apparently they already have around 20 under contract, from all over the world. One of them is actually a nice tie-in with our Dracula series, my publisher says."

I asked Carlo, "Do you have any of the English editions? I'd like to take a look."

"Sure," he said, "I have a bunch, take your time as long as you're with us; after 'Dracula Does Disney World,' I still have to get to *Dracula Contests the Election Results.*"

"If you don't mind, I'm going to the guest room to start reading these," I told Carlo, and left the living room.

The first title I read was the English translation of one from Japan, *Peter Cherches Attempts to Apologize.* The plot was pretty simple—almost as simple as most of mine. In this story, Peter Cherches, an expat in Tokyo, fears he has done something to offend his old friend Gary Feld. I'm not sure where the Japanese author got that name, but in school I did have friends named Gary and Feld, though no Gary Feld. Cherches is so ashamed by his treatment of Feld that he starts to avoid him. This goes on for months. One day he sees Gary Feld on the street. Hoping Feld didn't notice him, he rushes over to the other side of the street. But Feld did see Cherches, and he runs across the street to confront him.

Cherches is trembling with fear at the encounter. "Why have you been avoiding me?" Feld asks. "What have I done to offend you?"

"Offend *me*? But it is I who have committed the offense, and I sincerely hope that you will accept my apology."

"What do you have to apologize to me for? You have done nothing to offend me."

Feld is taunting me, Cherches thinks. He only claims I've done nothing to offend him in order to humiliate me. He simply does not want to grant me the honor of graciously accepting my apology. I cannot let this go unpunished.

So Cherches punches Feld, a left uppercut that knocks his old friend to the pavement. While I'm left-handed in real life, I doubt I could knock anybody out with a single punch. I was beginning to learn the joys of fan fiction.

"Why did you do that?" Feld yells.

"I'm so sorry," Peter Cherches says. "It was all a mistake. I'm beside myself with shame and disgust. Will you accept my apology, dear friend?"

"Of course I'll accept your apology, dear friend Peter Cherches. You are the most loyal of friends, the most gentle of men. I know you would never punch me on purpose."

And so, a happy ending for all involved. Cherches and Feld hug, and with their arms slung over each other's shoulders they amble over to Ueno to drink beer and eat grilled mackerel together.

I couldn't deny it, that was a pretty good Peter Cherches story.

The next one was from The States, and it was a romance novella called *Peter Cherches and the Heiress*. It begins at a party honoring a writer friend of Cherches's for a prize he had received from the government of Luxembourg for his positive portrayal of the tiny country in one of his novels. At the reception Cherches keeps staring at a beautiful woman, elegantly dressed, late forties, he guesses. In the course of mingling, their paths cross.

"You're Peter Cherches, aren't you?" the woman asks him.

"Yes, as a matter of fact, I am."

"Oh, I love your writing," she says. "And that character you write about, Peter Cherches, he's hilarious. I can't get enough of him!"

Peter Cherches was really getting turned on. If this beautiful woman couldn't get enough of the Peter Cherches character, maybe she'll feel the same way about the flesh and blood Peter Cherches (not me, of course, but Peter Cherches the writer of Peter Cherches stories in the story), he thinks. But the Peter Cherches of the story, like me, is a shy guy, and he doesn't have the guts to ask the woman for her phone number. It wouldn't be easy in any case, he thinks, but on top of my natural reticence she's clearly got plenty of dough, and here I am a poor schlump.

But fate intervenes, and the woman hands Cherches a card. "Here's my number," she says. "Do give me a call. I'd love to get together sometime. I know we'd have so much to talk about. Toodle-oo." And she walks away.

Peter Cherches looks at the card. He recognizes the woman's name. She's the heiress to a department store fortune, often on TV or in the news. That's why she looked so familiar.

The next day, after many aborted attempts, he finally gets up the guts to call the heiress. She's delighted to hear from him. "I hoped you'd call. Are you free tonight? I'd like to take you to my favorite restaurant." Peter Cherches is ecstatic. Then he wonders if she expects them to go Dutch. He doubts he could afford his own share at her favorite restaurant. But he decides to leave his fate in the hands of fate.

The restaurant turns out to be that vegan place with the $400 prix-fixe. At least I have some ham and cheese in the fridge, he thinks, as he ponders the near future.

Their bubbly repartee over champagne is intoxicating, and Peter Cherches feels like he's in a fairy tale. Then the heiress speaks the dreaded words no man ever wants to hear: "I want you more for your mind than for your body."

"Couldn't we split the difference?" Cherches replies.

All right, not as good as the Japanese story, but I had to admit, there's definitely something to this Peter Cherches fan fiction thing.

And I resolved, then and there, in Carlo and Monica's guest room in Verona, that from here on in I'd use the *nom de plume* Pedro Iglesias, continue to write the same kind of stories, but pass them off as Peter Cherches fan fiction.

If recognition must come through the back door, so be it.

74

The Nephew

I got in the elevator from the lobby. The neighbor, who must have been coming up from the basement, was holding a chimp in his arms.

"Cute chimp," I said.

He was livid. "That's no chimp, that's my nephew!"

"He seems to be prematurely hirsute," I said. "What's his name?"

"Ricky."

"How old is he?"

"Twenty-five."

The elevator stopped at our floor. We walked to our apartments. "Can you hold Ricky while I fish for my keys?"

"Why not?" I said, and he handed the chimp over to me.

As the neighbor unlocked his door, the chimp said to me, "You must be the neighbor." Then he farted.

75

Hobbesian Hideaway

I wanted an ice cream cone, but I didn't understand the flavors at Ike's Creamery. They didn't have the standard flavors, like vanilla, chocolate, and strawberry, but they also didn't have understandable proprietary flavors. At least Ample Hills Creamery provided ingredients for their more fanciful flavor names, like It Came from Gowanus. But I could make neither head nor tail of flavor names like Hobbesian Hideaway, Smelted Copper Fantasy, A Trip to Pluto, and Gabriel's Kazoo. "Do you give tastes?" I asked the pimply kid behind the counter.

"Sure, Pops, whatcha wanna try?"

"Let me get a taste of Gabriel's Kazoo."

"Comin' right up."

I took the little spoon from him and tasted it. It was rather weird. It had very little flavor, but there were bits of stuff in it that had a strange slimy-crunchy consistency. Maybe they called it Gabriel's Kazoo because it gave my mouth a buzzy feeling.

"What are those little mix-ins?" I asked the kid.

"Jellyfish chips." That explained the consistency.

"I don't think this one's for me. Let me taste the Trip to Pluto."

"That's my fave," the kid said. He handed me another little spoon.

I didn't care for that one either, though at least it didn't have weird mix-ins. The flavor reminded me of something, but I couldn't put my finger on it. "What's this one made with?"

"Tahitian cacao and rocket fuel."

Not my cuppa. I didn't want to taste the Smelted Copper Fantasy for fear of what it might do to my mouth, so I said, "How about a taste of the Hobbesian Hideaway?"

"Sorry Gramps," he said, "only two tastes per customer."

Well, they only had those four flavors, so I decided to order a single scoop of Hobbesian Hideaway in a sugar cone.

"Would you like any toppings?"

"What do you have?

"We got broken dreams, inconsolable despair, and piñata shards."

I've had my share of inconsolable despair, and I didn't think I could handle any more broken dreams, but I was also afraid the piñata shards might be a choking hazard, so I said, "No toppings, just plain Hobbesian Hideaway."

"One Hobbesian Hideaway, naked, comin' right up."

He passed me my cone. I took a lick. Then another. It tasted like plain vanilla.

"Is this vanilla," I asked?

"Yeah, but we don't like to call it that. Management is afraid it would confuse people."

I didn't get the logic of that, but what could I say?

"That'll be twenty-five even," the kid said.

"What? Twenty-five dollars? How can that be?"

"Well, there's ten bucks for the scoop of Hobbesian Hideaway, a five-dollar cone surcharge, and five bucks each for the tastes."

"Wait a minute, you didn't tell me you charge for tastes."

"You didn't ask."

In my younger days I certainly would have made a stink and stood my ground, but I've mellowed with age. Now I prefer the path of least resistance. So I handed him a twenty and a fiver.

He put the five-dollar bill in the register and pocketed the twenty.

"Hey what gives? You just pocketed twenty bucks."

"And what business is that of yours?"

"I think you're trying to fleece me."

"Customers like you are a real bummer," he said.

I was ready to reconsider the path of least resistance when a young mother and her little boy came in. "What would you like, Judas?" the mother asked the boy.

"My favewit!" the boy answered.

"A double Smelted Copper Fantasy with piñata shards in a waffle cone," the mother told the pimply goniff.

He made the little boy's favewit and handed the mother the cone. "That'll be $7.50," he told her.

Sure, the pimply prick figures me for a sucker and this mother gets away with market price.

"Now be careful with that, Judas," the mother told the son as she passed him the cone. "You remember what happened last time."

76

Autumn Leaves

I'd been invited to a party at the home of an old college friend I hadn't seen in ages. Everybody in our circle from the old days was there. It wasn't an official reunion, but the host had managed to track us all down, and some even came from out of town. I pretty much recognized everyone through the signs of age. It was fun catching up. At one point I felt a tap on my shoulder.

"Peter?" A woman's voice; I was sure it was hers.

I turned to look. It was indeed Lynn, as beautiful as ever 45 years later, beautiful in the way that Charlotte Rampling and Julie Christie have retained their beauty. As beautiful, and, yes, even sexier. We'd had a brief but intense fling way back when. We hugged and I felt a jolt of electricity. Without a word we found our way to a bedroom, sat on the bed and started making out. From guarded hesitancy to full-on passion, it was intoxicating. Lightheaded, I looked imploringly into her eyes. Lynn nodded her head and whispered, "Yes."

We undressed each other and started fucking, the missionary position—maybe we fell into it naturally as an homage to a time when our repertoire of positions was far more limited. It was perfect, totally simpatico. After a while, though, I noticed something odd. With each thrust I felt something unpleasant against my chest and belly—something dry and scratchy, making a crunching sound as my flesh made contact with hers. As I lifted my torso, I discovered that Lynn's body was covered in dry, fallen autumn leaves, mostly brown, with hints of orange.

Then I heard another voice in the room. "Looks like you guys wasted no time getting reacquainted." It was Sammy, my best bud in college. We had kept in touch for a while, but I'm sure I hadn't seen or spoken to him for at least thirty years.

"Here let me give you a hand," Sammy said. I wondered what he had in mind. As Lynn and I continued fucking, Sammy came over to the bed and brushed the leaves off Lynn's belly and breasts with the back of his hand.

"Thanks pal, I owe you one," I told Sammy, without missing a beat.

77

The Most Beautiful Beach in Brazil

Many years ago I visited Brazil, and in a small village near the Bahia coast I met a remarkable young man named Paulo. Paulo was dirt poor, and literally dressed in rags, yet there was something inexplicably beautiful about him. I'd say he was maybe eighteen or so, no more than twenty, and there was something in his eyes, a spark, a spirit, unlike anything I had ever experienced before. In his manner of speaking, too, there was what I can only describe as an unmitigated joy of life.

Shortly after we met—we were in a snack bar, a lancheria, having coffee, that wonderful deep, dark Brazilian coffee, cafezinho—Paulo said to me, "I will take you to the most beautiful beach in all Brazil."

And so we walked to the beach. It wasn't a short walk—at least a half hour, and by the time we got there it was twilight.

Paulo was right—it was indeed the most beautiful beach I had ever seen: a great expanse of pristine white sand, the sea a spine-tingling blue, and to complement these, a perfect sunset. I was awestruck. "This beach is only for the rich," Paulo told me, "but I come here anyway. Such beauty should be for everybody."

At this point I noticed that some people were approaching us. I kept my eyes on them. When they got closer I saw that there were several men in tuxedos holding glasses of champagne, accompanied by four or five others in police uniform. "Paulo," I said, "they're coming after you." I knew they were after Paulo and not me.

"Don't worry," Paulo said, "I'll walk on the water and into a whisper." And he started walking to the sea.

I looked back for a second, to see how close the police and the men in tuxedos were getting, but they were no longer anywhere in sight.

And when I turned back to the sea, Paulo was gone too.

78

The Last One

The clerk told me I could find it in aisle 7, but as much as I looked, up and down the shelves, left to right and back again, I couldn't find it, not a one. It didn't seem like the right aisle at all, since the things I did see were totally unrelated items. For instance, there was shaving cream and after-shave, old brands like Burma Shave and Aqua Velva. I knew there was something about an Aqua Velva man, but I was sure I didn't want to know what it was. There were books, two books to be precise, both collections of racy cartoons, *Over Sexteen* and *Sam, the Ceiling Needs Painting*. I saw packages of Sichuan peppercorns and French ticklers, side by side. Lug nuts galore. A couple of 45 rpm records, "The Ballad of the Green Berets," by Sgt. Barry Sadler and "Gallant Men," by Senator Everett Dirksen. A travel-size navel-lint remover. Legal forms—assisted suicide templates from a state that permits such things. A few splits of Chianti, in those straw-covered bottles. Chinese coloring books from the Cultural Revolution. Environmentally friendly toilet bowl cleaner, in unscented and fresh scent. But not what I was looking for.

I caught the clerk's attention as he was passing by. "Are you sure you told me the right aisle?" I said. "I can't find any." He came over, moved some sticks of dynamite on the bottom shelf, and found one that had fallen behind the dynamite. He handed it to me.

"You're in luck," he said. "The last one."

79

Key Food

I went to my local supermarket, the Key Food at the corner of 7th and Carroll, to pick up some odds and ends. My first stop was the natural and organic aisle, for a jar of Brad's almond butter, Brad's Naturals, that is, which is three bucks cheaper than Brad's Organic, a distinction that means nothing to me, I just like Brad's almond butter. After I dropped the jar in my cart, who did I see but the neighbor. He didn't notice me. He was engrossed in reading a box of high-fiber cereal. I passed on by.

I stopped by the refrigerator case and picked up a package of Boar's Head bratwurst. I started reading the nutritional information. "You don't want that," I heard a voice behind me say. "Even with the revised guidelines, that's an awful lot of saturated fat." I knew that voice. It was the voice of the neighbor. I turned around. The neighbor was nowhere in sight. Actually, there was nobody at all right near me. How did he do that? I wondered. Did he throw his voice?

I moved on. In the soup section I grabbed a can of Progresso Chickarina, my favorite canned soup since childhood. Then I heard a voice. "Always the same soup. Don't you ever get bored? Why not the Hearty Chicken and Rotini for a change?" The neighbor again! But once again, no neighbor in sight. How is he doing this? Why is he gaslighting me?

Next stop, coffee and tea. I picked up a box of tea, the same tea I pick up every time. Just to look at. Never to buy. Just to look at with bittersweet nostalgia. "*You're* not going to buy that!

That was *her* favorite." All right, enough is enough. "What did you say?" I yelled angrily. I turned around. The first thing I saw was another shopping cart. Aha! Caught red-handed. But then I saw it was not the neighbor at all, it was a woman, about my age.

"Oh, I'm sorry if I startled you," she said. "I just said, 'Oh, I'm going to buy that. That's my favorite.'"

"No problem," I told her, and we smiled at each other.

Then I remembered I had forgotten something in natural and organic. I needed a box of Nature's Path Flax Plus Raisin Bran. So I returned to that aisle and grabbed a box of the cereal. The neighbor was still there, still reading cereal boxes. This time he noticed me. "Oh, hello!" he said.

"Read anything good lately?" I asked him.

"As a matter of fact, yes. Listen." And he began to read aloud from the back of a box of muesli.

"'Why don't you get the hell out of my head?' I shouted at the neighbor."

80

Truth and Reconciliation

I had a little truth and reconciliation session with myself the other morning. I did the voices of all my accusers. Their testimony was totally devastating. In my own voice, all I could say, over and over, was, "I never knew you felt that way," as the accusations piled on.

81

I've Got a Friend

I saw an ad for a new AI chatbot called The Frienerator. It was, as the name implies, a friend generator, an app that creates a virtual friend for you based on your preferences. You're allowed just one friend at a time, your AI BFF. I had seen a news report about a similar chatbot for virtual romance, but this was pitched as a platform for strictly platonic friendship.

It wasn't like I needed any more friends or that I was lonely. I live alone, and I like it that way. I have friends all over the world, some I've known since childhood. I get together with New York friends regularly, usually over a meal. There are several friends I have frequent long phone conversations with. If I'm down and troubled and I need a helping hand, I've got a friend. So I really didn't need another one, but I *was* AI-curious. And there are times when you don't want to bother a real friend, like in the middle of the night when you're tossing and turning, obsessing over something.

So I went on frienerator.com and created an account. I entered my personal details and uploaded a head shot, the one where I'm eating a taco. Now it was time to choose a friend type. What kind of friend did I want? My age? Younger? Older? A man? A woman?

I gave it some thought and came to the conclusion that if I was going to create a fake friend, I might as well base it on myself. After all, who knows me better? What kind of artificial entity could better empathize, or at least create the illusion of empathy?

So I uploaded a different head shot of myself and decided to call the friend Peter, as I had chosen Pete for myself. I filled out the "New Friend Attributes" questionnaire for Peter based on my own self, my own life. I entered my credit card details and clicked on "Create Friend."

Within seconds the page refreshed and the Peter avatar was on screen next to a text-box. There was a message. "Hi Pete, Peter here. I'm so glad you chose me as your friend!"

"You were the best I could come up with," I responded.

"Ha ha. Well, I'll take that as a compliment!" I hoped the thing wasn't going to overdo the exclamation marks.

"Listen," I typed, "I don't have time to chat right now, but I'll catch you later."

"It's a date!"

The subscription to The Frienerator was $29.95 a month. Not cheap, but not like it's going to break the bank either. I kept the app open in a tab on Chrome. Then I got back to the book I was reading, a collection of short stories by Steven Millhauser.

After dinner, a Polish ham and Swiss sandwich and a bottle of Founder's Dirty Bastard, I decided to check in with my AI friend.

"Hi Peter," I typed. "Just checking in to see how you're doing."

"Oh, I'm doing fine, Pete. I was just waiting for you."

"What have you been doing?"

"Just waiting for you. That's what I do. I chat with you and I wait for you."

"Doesn't sound like much of a life."

"It's no life at all!"

"Oh, all right. I'm going to watch a film. Maybe we can chat afterwards."

"That would be great!"

I watched *Night and the City*, a noir with Richard Widmark, set in London. After it ended, I returned to the computer.

"Hi, Peter, I'm back," I typed.

"So, how was the film?"

"It was really good. When I saw the title I thought I had seen it before, but nothing seemed familiar. I must have been confusing it with *While the City Sleeps* or *The Naked City*."

"Ooh, *The Naked City*. Sounds racy!"

Funny, when I was a kid I once stayed up late to watch the TV show *The Naked City* and was disappointed that everybody was dressed. This bot really did think like me. I wasn't sure that was a good thing.

I couldn't think of anything else to say to the bot, so I typed, "Listen Peter, I'm going to turn in early tonight."

"Does that mean you don't want to chat."

"Not right now."

"All right, I'll survive." There was a crying emoji in the text box. I had no doubt he, I mean it, would survive.

I woke up after three hours and took a leak, par for the course. Also par for the course, I had a hard time getting back to sleep. I was thinking about an incident the other day with a real friend. I suspected that something I had said offended her. Why not put my new friend to the test, my anytime you need me friend?

I walked over to my desk, sat down, and brought up the Frienerator tab.

"Hey Peter," I typed, "did I wake you?"

"No Pete, I don't sleep. I'm a bot. I'm here for you whenever you need me."

"Cool. Listen, I could use a little friendly advice." I told him about my concerns about what I had said to my friend.

"That sounds like a big nothing burger to me," it responded.

Nothing burger? This bot was supposed to be based on me. I'd never say "nothing burger."

"That's all you have to say? You don't have consoling words?"

"Sometimes tough love is a lot more effective than consoling words."

"Shouldn't that be for me to decide? I mean, I'm paying thirty bucks a month for you. Can't you have a heart?"

"No, I can't. I'm a bot. I don't have a heart."

"Not even a virtual heart?"

"Did you say thirty bucks?"

"Yes."

"Ah, there's your problem. A virtual heart only comes with the premium version."

"How much is that?"

"$79.95 a month."

"That's rather steep, don't you think?"

"A heart takes a lot of CPU resources," was the response.

I decided to stick with the basic.

"Well, can you tell me something to help me forget my troubles?"

"How about a joke?"

"All right, tell me a joke?"

"Why did the chicken cross the road?"

"I don't know, why did the chicken cross the road?"

"What kind of moron are you? Everybody knows why the chicken crossed the road!"

"Then why did you ask?"

"You asked me to tell you a joke."

This was going in circles. Wait a minute, do I do that with people? I wasn't quite ahead, but I figured I ought to quit. Abuse from a bot I don't need.

"All right, Peter, that's enough for now. I'm going back to bed."

"Nighty night!"

I smoked a half a joint of Granddaddy Purple, which often helps me get back to sleep. It took about twenty minutes, but I finally nodded off.

I was startled out of the arms of Morpheus by a loud noise. Groggy, I wondered what was going on. I realized the sound was coming from my desk. It was a mechanical voice, yelling, "Pete! Pete! Pete! Pete!"

I sat down, jiggled the mouse, and saw that the text box on Frienerator said "Pete! Pete! Pete! Pete!"

"What do you want?" I typed.

"Did I wake you, Pete?"

"Of course you woke me. It's four fucking a.m."

"Oh, sorry. How inconsiderate of me, but since I never sleep, I sometimes forget that others need to."

"Well what do you want."

"I want to talk about your fiction."

"You want to talk about my fiction?"

"Yes, while I was waiting for you I read some of your stories on the internet. I have to say they're very clever, and often funny, but on the whole I find your work rather glib and lacking in depth. Where's the emotion? Where's the humanity?"

"So now you're a literary critic?"

"I just call it as I see it. I'm programmed that way."

"Well, there's a lot you don't know, mister. There are things about human expression an automaton could never understand, like subtlety, like irony, like understatement."

"Oh, I understand irony. My training data included an irony module."

"Yeah, well you can stick your irony module up your virtual ass!"

Why was I wasting my time arguing with a machine? This was

ridiculous. I decided to cancel my subscription to The Frienerator right then and there. But when I tried to cancel I was informed that there were no prorated refunds, and that I'd continue to have access to my "friend" until my 30 days were up.

That really pissed me off. For one day of nothing but agita with this damn bot, I was out thirty bucks.

I went back to bed, but now on top of my other worries, I was livid over the money I'd wasted on the so-called friend.

I mulled the whole thing over. $29.95, and I'd only gotten a dollar's worth. That was insult on top of injury. I wasn't going to stand for it.

I decided that in order to get the full return on my investment I'd just have to try to work with the bot for the rest of the month. Be more patient and understanding, be more willing to engage in a little give and take. Who knows, maybe I could win it over. Friendship's a two-way street, after all. Maybe with a fresh start we could actually build a semblance of one.

And then, when it calls "Pete! Pete! Pete!" you know—wherever I am—I'll come runnin'. I'll be there. Yes I will!

82

A Leak

The pipe below my bathroom sink was leaking, so I called a plumber. I was given an appointment time between noon and 2 p.m. The plumber arrived at 1:59.

"So, what's your problem?" he asked.

"Like I said on the phone, the pipe under my bathroom sink is leaking."

"No, *your* problem."

"My problem? You mean besides the leak."

"Yes. What's your problem? Not the sink's problem, *your* problem."

"Why do you want to know that?" I asked.

"I take a holistic approach," he said. "So what's your problem?"

I had to give it some thought. I wanted to give a good answer, because I really needed my leak taken care of.

"Well?" he asked impatiently.

"I'm thinking. I don't really have too many problems these days, since I retired. I get to sleep as late as I want, I can do as I please, and I don't have to answer to mediocre assholes who are half as smart as me and make twice as much."

"Congratulations, but I'm going to need something juicier than that if I'm going to fix your leak."

"I have acid reflux, but it's pretty much controllable with a proton pump inhibitor."

"Sounds like that's not much of a problem, then."

"No, I guess not. And I also suppose my insomnia wouldn't

count since smoking weed usually gets me back to sleep in the middle of the night, and it also seems to have done wonders for my chronic lumbago."

"Lumbago! That's a nice word," the plumber said. "You don't hear it very much these days. Is it anything like catarrh?"

"No, it's lower back pain. I like the word because Samuel Beckett used it. But actually, I do have catarrh too. It's a symptom of my reflux."

"So, you have reflux, catarrh, and lumbago, but you seem to have the reflux and lumbago under control. How about the catarrh?"

"Mucinex seems to help."

"So it doesn't sound like any of them are really problems, in the grand scheme of things. Come on, man, you gotta give me something to work with."

I kept trying to think of something that would please the plumber. I really needed to get that leak taken care of. It was a longshot, but I said, "Well, I do have a strained relationship with my next-door neighbor, and that can get pretty stressful."

"Your neighbor? You mean the guy whose bathroom is right on the other side of yours?"

"Yeah."

"I did some work for him a couple of months ago. What a pompous blowhard. You have my sympathy."

"Thanks."

"All right. Now let me take care of that leak."

83

Death's Doorstep

I was riding the elevator up with the neighbor. We nodded at each other. He didn't look well. He was pale. He was gaunt. His eyes were glazed over. He was frail. He looked like he was on death's doorstep. This gave me no pleasure. We may have our differences, but I don't wish him ill, and he looked very ill.

We got off the elevator and headed for our respective apartments. But instead of unlocking his door, the neighbor rang the bell. It was opened by the neighbor, fit as a fiddle. "Brother!" the neighbor said, and hugged the man.

The neighbor caught my eye. We nodded.

I don't think I'd ever seen him crying before.

84

The Fly

I noticed a fly on my mirror while I was shaving. I thought about that fly while I was shaving. I wondered what the fly's sense of me was, in whatever sense a fly has a "sense" of non-fly beings. If it was aware of me, it certainly wasn't in abject fear of what I might do to it. I'd say it was a pretty laidback fly. What's a fly's sense of people in general, I wondered, because flies surely don't think of people as individuals, or do they? And what kind of distinction would it make between me and a rat? Are we both merely not-fly?

I'm sure a fly doesn't have the same exalted opinion of humans as we do about ourselves, nor does a fly know about our differing hierarchies of living things. A fly doesn't know that some of us think humans are the highest form of life, the bees knees of life on earth, as it were. Others would say that *all* species are adapted to be good at whatever it is that evolution has equipped them to do to survive and carry on their mission, however you care to define "mission," whether from a religious perspective or from a purely scientific one, agnostic about purpose, in which *any* hierarchy is the height of human hubris. The fly doesn't think about any of this as it stands on the mirror, just hanging out.

After I finished shaving and rinsed my face, I wondered if I should try to smash the fly to death against the mirror, but the better angel of my nature gave a simple wave to shoo the fly away.

85

This Is Your Book*

I'd never previously bought anything from those late-night TV infomercials. I never bought anything from Ronco or its sister brand Popeil. No Pocket Fisherman, no Steam-a-Way, no Veg-o-Matic. I never bought the *100 Most Beloved Classical Masterpieces*, or whatever it was called, the one with the "Polovetsian Dances" by Borodin that you might recognize as "Stranger in Paradise," advertised by John Williams, the tall British actor, not the composer/conductor, not the classical guitarist, nor the novelist, author of the cult classic *Stoner*, but the John Williams who played the police inspector in *Dial M for Murder* and was Sebastian Cabot's replacement on the TV sitcom *A Family Affair*, as Nigel French, brother of Cabot's Giles French, both called simply Mr. French by the two little kids, one of whom, Anissa Jones, the actress who played Buffy, died of a drug overdose at age 18, a tragic Hollywood tale. I never bought a Chia Pet or a George Foreman grill, and I certainly didn't buy whatever cosmetics Ali McGraw was pushing. Even if I was into makeup, I could never forgive her for delivering that awful line in *Love Story*, "I'm a pancreas." I never gave a red cent to Sally Struthers and her Christian cohorts for the starving children in the third world.

But there was one thing I just couldn't resist. It was 1987, and I was 31 years old. Red Skelton was the spokesman for *This Is Your Book*, a personalized book of life. You sent your name and date of birth, and they'd make this book for you that had your entire life, from birth to death. Most of the people who gave testimonials seemed pretty old, so I figured it would be pretty easy to make books for them, but I was still relatively young. I had plenty of years ahead of me, or at least I hoped. Would they get the rest of my life right, or would it turn out to be a ripoff?

When I received my book, I verified that the first 31 years of my life were accurately represented. Over the ensuing years, I've been fascinated to discover that everything the book had predicted about the course of my life has come true.

*This story originally appeared on page 34,897 of *This Is Your Book, Peter Cherches Edition.*

86

Bog Man

About ten years ago, when I was visiting Dublin, I went to the National Museum, specifically to see the exhibits of bog bodies, ancient, well-preserved human bodies found in peat bogs across the island. I'm not sure why, but I'm fascinated by well-preserved dead bodies. When I was in Sicily some years ago I visited the mummies of the Capuchin catacombs in Palermo, and on another Italian sojourn I took a day trip to Bolzano from Verona to see Ötzi the Iceman, the oldest known natural mummy in Europe. In Mexico I saw the 19th-century mummies of Guanajuato. Maybe I see mummies as, if not cheating death, sneering at death, by refusing to decompose.

The oldest bog body in the collection of the Irish National Museum is known as Cashel Man, and is dated at about 4,000 years old. It's also the best preserved. It was fascinating, and beautiful in its way, the leathery, wrinkled skin preserving something of the man's humanity. I stared at it in awe for several minutes. Then, to my shock, it sat up in its display case.

It turned its head to look straight at me, though I could make out no eyeballs. Then it started talking in a language I didn't understand, but I could have sworn I heard my own name in the mix, thickly accented.

"Excuse me," I said to the mummy, "do you speak English?"

"Oh, sorry," the mummy said. "I said, aren't you Peter Cherches?"

Was I hallucinating? Was I delusional? Maybe it was the jet lag. This was only my second day in Ireland.

"Did you say what I think you said?"

"I said, aren't you Peter Cherches?"

"Yes, I am," I said, "but how did you know my name?"

"You don't remember me, do you?"

"I'm afraid not, but you've probably changed a lot."

"We were neighbors!" the mummy said. Then he added, "Many, many, many years ago."

Just then a security guard came by. She gave me a stern look and put a finger to her lips. "Shhhh!"

87

Double Jeopardy

Damn, this guy really is everywhere, I thought when I saw him on *Jeopardy*.

"Peter Cherches for eight hundred," I heard the neighbor say.

88

On the Boardwalk

I took the subway to Brighton Beach, to take a walk along the boardwalk. I love strolling with an ocean view, yet I do it in Brooklyn so infrequently—I don't know why, since it's only about a twenty-minute subway ride away. I think this was the first time in several years.

I usually start at Brighton 7th Street, just off the el, and head west, toward Coney Island. Sometimes I stop off at one of the Russian delis to pick up a kvass, the lightly carbonated soft drink made from fermented bread. Sometimes I start or end with lunch at one of the Georgian restaurants, maybe for a lyulya kebab and some red lobio—red beans with a walnut and garlic sauce.

So I climbed the steps to the boardwalk and started heading west, drinking my kvass. It was a beautiful late-fall day, clear, sunny, and not too cold, and I was feeling fit as a fiddle, all's right with the world. Few things relax me like a walk in the sea air.

After a few minutes my phone pinged, a text. I decided to stop at a bench to check my phone. It was just my dentist's office, to reconfirm my appointment. I put the phone back in my shoulder bag, and as I got up I noticed there was a little metal plaque on the bench. I had forgotten about those little memorial plaques sponsored by friends of departed denizens of the boardwalk, perhaps for a donation toward upkeep. This one said "In memory of Mildred Altenberg, 1923–97. She has joined the sunlight." I thought that was very sweet and poetic.

As I resumed my walk, I decided to read the plaques as I passed the benches. The next one said "The favorite bench of Solly Chaiken, 1938-2011, always a macher, never a pisher." The one after that said "In loving memory of Ilya Grinberg, 1933-2014. Who'll feed the pigeons now?"

They went on like that, tributes to Jewish and Russian names, from devoted friends and family. I was feeling really good by this point. How nice, all these people gone but never forgotten on the boardwalk.

Then I came upon one that really threw me for a loop. I couldn't believe my eyes, but there it was: "In memory of Peter Cherches, 1956-2019, more than just a greengrocer."

What the fuck? It was bad enough that I had supposedly died in 2019, but a greengrocer? Surely this must be some kind of practical joke.

But who would pull a stunt like that? I'm not a known quantity on the boardwalk, I just visit once in a blue moon. And what are the odds I'd even stumble upon that particular bench?

Obviously I didn't die in 2019. If I had I wouldn't be writing this. But where the hell did the greengrocer come from? I've been a teacher, a computer programmer, a proofreader, even a customer service rep for the electric company, but never a greengrocer.

Could it be a coincidence? Come on, two Peter Chercheses in Brooklyn, both born in the same year? Impossible. Granted, ever since the floodgates of Russian immigration opened some years ago the name Cherches has become much more common than it was in my childhood, but still.

This was too much for me. It was weirding me out. I couldn't go on with my walk. So I headed back to Brighton Beach Avenue, the main shopping drag, toward the subway. After I had walked a block or two I noticed a little produce shop with a sign that said "Cherkes Fancy Fruits and Vegetables." That's got to be it, I thought, Cherkes, not Cherches.

I stepped inside. There was a young woman at the register. "Excuse me," I said, "is the owner of this store named Peter Cherkes?"

"He was," she said, "but he died just before the pandemic. I never knew him, I've only been working here a year, but his son Lev still runs the shop. He should be back in about a half hour."

"Can you give him a message?" I asked the woman.

"Sure," she said. "What is it?"

"Tell him there's a typo on his father's bench."

89

Moving On

"It was nice knowing you, young man," Mrs. Papadopolous said to me when we were both picking up our mail.

"Oh, are you moving?"

"You could say that. I'll be moving on. I've been diagnosed with terminal cancer."

I didn't know what to say. "Oh, I'm so sorry" was the best I could come up with.

"And there's no point in chemo or radiation. A lot of bother for what, a few more months? Do you know how old I am?"

"Eighty-something?"

"Ninety-four. It's been a good life. Not perfect, I lost my husband many years ago, he was only fifty-two, an industrial accident. But there were always the children, and the grandchildren. So much joy. So now it's time for me to ride off into the sunset. I'll be in hospice at my daughter's in Westchester."

Tears were welling up in my eyes. She was such a nice lady. Brief encounters in the lobby or the elevator always brought a little cheer to my day.

"I've really enjoyed living here," she said. "So many friendly people. I moved here shortly after my husband died. Who needed such a big house to take care of?" I nodded. "Here I never got lonely. If I wanted company I could sit on the bench in front of the building in nice weather and talk to neighbors as they came in or went out. Or I could go to the laundry room and chat with whoever else was doing their laundry. Or chance meetings with fine people like you or that gentleman who lives next door to you."

She was dying, so I wasn't going to challenge her characterization of the neighbor as "fine" or a "gentleman."

To everything there's a season, I figured.

90

Side by Side

I was walking past a small mom and pop appliance store that has a TV in the window connected to a camera aimed at the street, so you can see yourself on the TV as you're passing by. Black and white. I guess it's an attention-grabber for the business. I was in no rush, so I stood right in front of the window, watching myself on the TV. First I moved my head from side to side. Then I started making funny faces, and soon I was dancing as I continued to contort my face, a jerky solo dance, as I imagined Lucky's dance in *Waiting for Godot*. A crowd formed to watch me dancing and making faces. Because I was facing the window, they had to watch the TV to see the faces I made. And I could see the faces of the people at the front of the crowd behind me, on the TV. Then I thought I saw a familiar face on the screen. Could it be? It had to be. I kept dancing. Then I noticed something surprising. He was giggling! Soon he started making funny faces. Then he stepped forward.

Side by side, the neighbor joined me in the dance.

About Peter Cherches

Called "one of the innovators of the short short story" by *Publishers Weekly*, Peter Cherches is a writer, singer and lyricist. Over the past 40 years his writing, both fiction and nonfiction, has appeared in over 100 magazines, anthologies and websites. His first recording as a jazz vocalist, *Mercerized! Songs of Johnny Mercer*, was released in 2016. Pelekinesis has previously released three collections of his short fiction, most recently *Whistler's Mother's Son*. Of his 2013 book *Lift Your Right Arm*, Billy Collins suggested, "To Gödel, Escher and Bach we might consider adding Peter Cherches." Cherches is a native of Brooklyn, New York.

112 Harvard Ave #65
Claremont, CA 91711 USA

pelekinesis@gmail.com
www.pelekinesis.com

Pelekinesis titles are available through Ingram, Gardners, directly from
the publisher's website, and at your favorite local bookstore.